# THE SHOOTING SCRIPT

# AMERICAN BEAUTY

SCREENPLAY AND AFTERWORD BY
## ALAN BALL

INTRODUCTION BY
## SAM MENDES

A Newmarket Shooting Script® Series Book
NEWMARKET PRESS • NEW YORK

## ACKNOWLEDGMENTS

The publisher wishes to thank the following people who made an invaluable contribution to this book: Alan Ball, Susan Bennett, Sharon Black, Joyce Brouwers, Andrew Cannava, Bruce Cohen and Dan Jinks, Tara B. Cook, Kristy Cox, Anne Globe, Margo Lane, Sam Mendes, Esperanza Perez, Boyd Peterson, Terry Press, Dorit Saines, Michael Vollman, and Stephanie Wheeler.

DreamWorks extends a special thanks to Esther Margolis, John Cook, Tom Perry, and the rest of the staff at Newmarket Press who believed in the project and worked at breakneck speed to make this book possible.

9 8 7 6 5 4 3 2 1

ISBN-13: 978-1-55704-404-4 (pb)
ISBN-10: 1-55704-404-X (pb)
ISBN: 1-55704-423-6 (hc)

Library of Congress Catalog-in-Publication Data is available upon request.

QUANTITY PURCHASES

Companies, professional groups, clubs, and other organizations may qualify for special terms when ordering quantities of this title. For information, write to Special Sales, Newmarket Press, 18 East 48th Street, New York, NY 10017; call (212) 832-3575 or 1-800-669-3903; FAX (212) 832-3629; or e-mail info@newmarketpress.com.
Website: www.newmarketpress.com

Manufactured in the United States of America.

# CONTENTS

# INTRODUCTION

## BY SAM MENDES

I first read *American Beauty* sitting on a plane traveling between Los Angeles and New York. I finished it, and read it again. I arrived in New York, called my agent, Beth, and told her that I wanted to make the movie. Then I read it again. Normally it was a trial for me to get through a script once, and I'd read this one three times back to back. I wanted to know why this was. So I read it again.

The strange thing was that at each reading the script seemed to be something else. It was a highly inventive black comedy. It was a mystery story with a genuine final twist. It was a kaleidoscopic journey through American suburbia, and a hugely visually articulate one at that. It was a series of love stories. It was about imprisonment in the cages we all make for ourselves and our hoped-for escape. It was about loneliness. It was about beauty. It was funny. It was angry, very angry sometimes. It was sad. One thing I was certain of, the script, like its characters, wasn't at all what it first appeared.

Our relationship with the characters shifted and changed. What was this man Lester doing? Acting like a spoiled child or raging against the dying of the light? His wife Carolyn? Furious and frigid, yet vulnerable and lost. Jane? Impassive, unreadable, but with a well of tenderness barely visible to the naked eye. And Ricky. His camera emotionlessly recording its subject or reaching out to touch it? In the end my feelings about the finished movie and the script are indivisible. I love it (I'm biased, of course), but I still don't know how it *works*. With me, and also I suspect with Alan, instinct was my strongest and only guide.

One thing I did know on those initial readings, however, was that the writer wasn't scared to leave the characters alone with themselves; he seemed to know them well enough to allow them that privilege. Indeed, many of my favorite passages from the finished movie involve these moments of solitariness, caught by the camera's impassive and uninflected gaze. Carolyn in the empty sale house, putting herself back together again; Jane studying her reflection in the mirror after her mother has hit her; Ricky similarly alone in his room cleaning the blood from his face; Angela sitting on the stairs crying, with the rain outside; and of course Lester gazing at the image of his family, seeing it all clearly as it were, at the moment before his own death. Indeed, the voice that hovers over the movie seems to be the ultimate spiritual extension of that: Lester at once alone and at peace with himself, yet missing, genuinely missing, his "little life."

The movie was, of course, to repeat the old adage, extensively reshaped in the cutting room. A framework involving Ricky and Jane being tried and convicted of Lester's murder seemed clever but a mite cynical and at odds with Lester's spirit taking wing. This was excised along with any indications of the Colonel's ambivalent sexual feelings and other signposts that softened the movie's unexpected plot twists and changes of tone. Other changes were not so considered. The scene with Ricky and Jane walking home down the avenue of trees, for example, was written at the last minute to save us money and time, and turned out better than the scene it replaced. But it would be wrong to suggest that the film was ever in need of major surgery: Alan wrote it from the heart as well as the head, and it made it onto the screen with remarkably little interference from outside forces, other than the constant and unstinting support of producers Dan Jinks and Bruce Cohen, its torch bearers from the very beginning.

Of course, a whole set of additional presences enriched the movie. The extraordinary artistry and humanity of cinematographer Conrad Hall, the beautiful music of Tom Newman, along with the work of countless others, not to mention the huge contributions made by Kevin, Annette, Chris, Allison, Peter, Wes, Thora, and Mena. Most of that remains for you to see on film, but some of it is even here: Carolyn's dialogue with herself at the dinner table, Lester's phone conversation at work, and a variety of other improvisations that Alan shaped and positioned and now remain as a testament to the sheer pleasure we took in rehearsing and shooting this film.

But in the end, without Alan's work on the original script, none of these people, myself included, would have taken this particular journey. And as I sit writing this in the dry, odorless L.A. sunshine, contemplating my twelve months working on the movie and looking forward to going home, I can only reflect on the power of the written word to change our little lives.

# AMERICAN BEAUTY

Screenplay by
Alan Ball

FADE IN:

INT. FITTS HOUSE - RICKY'S BEDROOM - NIGHT

On **VIDEO:** JANE BURNHAM lays in bed, wearing a tank top.
She's sixteen, with dark, intense eyes.

> JANE
> I need a father who's a role model, not
> some horny geek-boy who's gonna spray his
> shorts whenever I bring a girlfriend home
> from school.
>         (snorts)
> What a lame-o. Somebody really should put
> him out of his misery.

Her mind wanders for a beat.

> RICKY (O.C.)
> Want me to kill him for you?

Jane looks at us and sits up.

> JANE
>         (deadpan)
> Yeah, would you?

FADE TO BLACK.

FADE IN:

EXT. ROBIN HOOD TRAIL - EARLY MORNING

We're FLYING above suburban America, DESCENDING SLOWLY toward
a tree-lined street.

> LESTER (V.O.)
> My name is Lester Burnham. This is my
> neighborhood. This is my street. This...
> is my life. I'm forty-two years old. In
> less than a year, I'll be dead.

INT. BURNHAM HOUSE - MASTER BEDROOM - CONTINUOUS

We're looking down at a king-sized BED from OVERHEAD:

LESTER BURNHAM lies sleeping amidst expensive bed linens,
face down, wearing PAJAMAS. An irritating ALARM CLOCK RINGS.
Lester gropes blindly to shut it off.

> LESTER (V.O.)
> Of course, I don't know that yet.

CONTINUED:

He rolls over, looks up at us and sighs. He doesn't seem too thrilled at the prospect of a new day.

             LESTER (V.O.) (cont'd)
        And in a way, I'm dead already.

He sits up and puts on his slippers.

INT. BURNHAM HOUSE - MASTER BATH - MOMENTS LATER

Lester thrusts his face directly into a steaming hot shower.

ANGLE from outside the shower: Lester's naked body is silhouetted through the fogged-up glass door. It becomes apparent he is masturbating.

             LESTER (V.O.)
        (amused)
        Look at me, jerking off in the shower.
        (then)
        This will be the high point of my day.
        It's all downhill from here.

EXT. BURNHAM HOUSE - MOMENTS LATER

CLOSE on a single, dewy AMERICAN BEAUTY ROSE. A gloved hand with CLIPPERS appears and SNIPS the flower off.

CAROLYN BURNHAM tends her rose bushes in front of the Burnham house. A very well-put together woman of forty, she wears color-coordinated gardening togs and has lots of useful and expensive tools.

Lester watches her through a WINDOW on the first floor, peeping out through the drapes.

             LESTER (V.O.)
        That's my wife Carolyn. See the way the
        handle on those pruning shears matches
        her gardening clogs? That's not an
        accident.

EXT. JIMS' HOUSE - CONTINUOUS

In the fenced front yard of the house next door, a dog BARKS repeatedly. A MAN in a conservative suit (JIM #1) chastises the barking dog.

             JIM #1
        Hush, Bitsy. You hush. What is wrong?

             LESTER (V.O.)
        That's our next-door neighbor Jim.

                                          (CONTINUED)

CONTINUED:


A second MAN in a conservative suit (JIM #2) comes out of the
house.

                    LESTER (V.O.)
          And that's his lover, Jim.

                    JIM #2
               (re: barking dog)
          What in the world is wrong with her? She
          had a walk this morning.

                    JIM #1
          And a jerky treat.

                    JIM #2
          You spoil her.
               (sternly)
          Bitsy. No bark. Come inside. Now.

EXT. BURNHAM HOUSE - CONTINUOUS

Lester watches all this from the window.

                    CAROLYN
          Good morning, Jim!

Jim #1 walks toward the fence to greet Carolyn.

                    JIM #1
          Morning, Carolyn.

                    CAROLYN
               (overly friendly)
          I just love your tie! That color!

                    JIM #1
          I just love your roses. How do you get
          them to flourish like this?

                    CAROLYN
          Well, I'll tell you. Egg shells and
          Miracle Grow.

Jim #1 and Carolyn continue to chat, unaware that Lester is
watching them.

                    LESTER (V.O.)
          Man. I get exhausted just watching her.

Lester's POV: We can't hear what Jim and Carolyn are saying,
but she's overly animated, like a TV talk show host.


                                              (CONTINUED)

CONTINUED:

>           LESTER (V.O.)
>     She wasn't always like this. She used to
>     be happy. <u>We</u> used to be happy.

INT. BURNHAM HOUSE - JANE'S ROOM - CONTINUOUS

JANE is seated at her desk, working at her computer.

>           LESTER (V.O.)
>     My daughter Jane. Only child.

CLOSE on the COMPUTER MONITOR: A PERSONAL BANKING SOFTWARE
window suddenly disappears to reveal another window: a
PLASTIC SURGERY WEBSITE, featuring clinical "before" and
"after" photos of surgically augmented breasts.

>           LESTER (V.O.) (cont'd)
>     Janie's a pretty typical teenager. Angry,
>     insecure, confused. I wish I could tell
>     her that's all going to pass...

Outside, a CAR HORN BLARES. Jane stuffs items into her
BACKPACK.

>           LESTER (V.O.) (cont'd)
>     But I don't want to lie to her.

We HEAR the CAR HORN again from outside. Jane studies herself
in a mirror, then shifts to get a good profile of her
breasts.

EXT. BURNHAM HOUSE - CONTINUOUS

Carolyn stands next to a platinum-colored MERCEDES-BENZ
ML320, reaching in through the drivers' window to blow the
HORN again.

Jane shuffles out of the house, her backpack slung over her
shoulder.

>           CAROLYN
>     Jane. Honey. Are you trying to look
>     unattractive?

>           JANE
>     Yes.

>           CAROLYN
>     Well, congratulations. You've succeeded
>     admirably.

Jane gets in the car. Lester hurries out the front door,
carrying a BRIEFCASE.

                                          (CONTINUED)

CONTINUED:

                    CAROLYN (cont'd)
Lester, could you make me a little <u>later</u>,
please? Because I'm not quite late
enough.

Lester's briefcase suddenly springs open and his papers spill
all over the driveway. He drops to his knees to gather
everything.

                    JANE
Nice going, Dad.

Lester smiles sheepishly, trying to lighten the moment.

His POV: Carolyn looks down at us, contemptuous but also
bored, as if she gave up expecting anything more long ago.

                    LESTER (V.O.)
Both my wife and daughter think I'm this
gigantic loser, and... they're right.

INT. MERCEDES-BENZ ML320 - A SHORT TIME LATER

Carolyn is driving; Jane stares out the window. Lester is
asleep in the back seat.

                    LESTER (V.O.)
I <u>have</u> lost something. I'm not exactly
sure what it is, but I know I didn't
always feel this... sedated. But you know
what? It's never too late to get it back.

INT. OFFICE BUILDING - DAY

Lester sits at his workstation, a BEIGE CUBICLE surrounded by
IDENTICAL BEIGE CUBICLES. He's staring at a computer monitor
and talking on a HEADSET PHONE. The beleaguered expression on
his face is at odds with the light, friendly tone of his
voice.

                    LESTER
Hello, this is Lester Burnham from Media
Monthly magazine, I'm calling for Mr.
Tamblin, please?... Well, we're all under
a deadline here, uh, but you see, there
is some basic information about the
product launch that isn't even covered in
your press release and I... Yeah. Can I
ask you a question? Who is Tamblin? Does
he exist? 'Cause he doesn't ever seem to
come in... Yeah, okay, I'll leave my
number...

CONTINUED:

BRAD, a dapper man in his thirties, approaches and observes Lester, who is unaware of his presence.

>                    LESTER
>          It's 555 0199. Lester Burnham. Thank you!

Lester disconnects the call, obviously irritated.

>                    BRAD
>          Hey Les. You got a minute?

Lester turns around, smiling perfunctorily

>                    LESTER
>          For you, Brad? I've got five.

INT. BRAD'S OFFICE - MOMENTS LATER

Brad is seated behind his desk in his big corner office.

>                    BRAD
>          I'm sure you can understand our need to
>          cut corners around here.

Lester sits across from him, looking small and isolated.

>                    LESTER
>          Oh, sure. Times are tight, and you gotta
>          free up cash. Gotta spend money to make
>          money. Right?

>                    BRAD
>          Exactly. So...

Brad stands, ready to usher Lester out.

>                    LESTER
>               (blurts)
>          Like the time when Mr. Flournoy used the
>          company MasterCard to pay for that
>          hooker, and then she used the card
>          numbers and stayed at the St. Regis for,
>          what was it, like, three months?

>                    BRAD
>               (startled)
>          That's unsubstantiated gossip.

>                    LESTER
>          That's fifty thousand dollars. That's
>          somebody's salary. That's somebody who's
>          gonna get fired because Craig has to pay
>          women to fuck him!

CONTINUED:

                    BRAD
          Jesus. Calm down. Nobody's getting fired
          yet. That's why we're having everyone
          write out a job description, mapping out
          in detail how they contribute. That way,
          management can assess who's valuable and--

                    LESTER
          Who's expendable.

                    BRAD
          It's just business.

                    LESTER
               (angry)
          I've been writing for this magazine for
          fourteen years, Brad. You've been here
          how long, a whole month?

                    BRAD
               (frank)
          I'm one of the good guys, Les. I'm trying
          to level with you. This is your one
          chance to save your job.

Lester stares at him, powerless.

EXT. BURNHAM HOUSE - LATE AFTERNOON

A MOVING VAN is parked in front of the COLONIAL HOUSE next
door to the Burnhams'. Movers carry furniture toward the
house.

The Mercedes-Benz pulls into the Burnham driveway. Carolyn
drives, Lester is in the passenger seat.

                    CAROLYN
          --there is no decision, you just write
          the damn thing!

                    LESTER
          You don't think it's weird and kinda
          fascist?

                    CAROLYN
          Possibly. But you don't want to be
          unemployed.

                    LESTER
          Oh, well, let's just all sell our souls
          and work for Satan, because it's more
          convenient that way.

CONTINUED:

> CAROLYN
> Could you be just a little bit <u>more</u>
> dramatic, please, huh?

As they get out of the car, Carolyn scopes out the MOVERS next door.

> CAROLYN (cont'd)
> So we've finally got new neighbors. You
> know, if the Lomans had let <u>me</u> represent
> them, instead of--
> (heavy disdain)
> --"The Real Estate King," that house
> would never have sat on the market for
> six months.

She heads into the house, followed by Lester.

> LESTER
> Well, they were still mad at you for
> cutting down their sycamore.

> CAROLYN
> <u>Their</u> sycamore? C'mon! A substantial
> portion of the root structure was on our
> property. You know that. How can you call
> it <u>their</u> sycamore? I wouldn't have the
> heart to just cut down something if it
> wasn't partially mine, which of course it
> was.

<u>INT. BURNHAM HOUSE - DINING ROOM - LATER THAT NIGHT</u>

We HEAR EASY-LISTENING MUSIC.

Lester, Carolyn and Jane are eating dinner by CANDLELIGHT.
RED ROSES are bunched in a vase at the center of the table.
Nobody makes eye contact, or even seems aware of anybody
else's presence, until...

> JANE
> Mom, do we always have to listen to this
> elevator music?

> CAROLYN
> (considers)
> No. No, we don't. As soon as you've
> prepared a nutritious yet savory meal
> that <u>I'm</u> about to eat, you can listen to
> whatever you like.

A long beat. Lester suddenly turns to Jane.

(CONTINUED)

CONTINUED:

                    LESTER
So Janie, how was school?

                    JANE
    (suspicious)
It was okay.

                    LESTER
Just okay?

                    JANE
No, Dad. It was spec-tac-ular.

A beat.

                    LESTER
Well, you want to know how things went at
my job today?

Now she looks at him as if he's lost his mind.

                    LESTER
They've hired this efficiency expert,
this really friendly guy named Brad, how
perfect is that? And he's basically there
to make it seem like they're justified in
firing somebody, because they couldn't
just come right out and say that, could
they? No, no, that would be too...
honest. And so they've asked us--
    (off her look)
--you couldn't possibly care any less,
could you?

Carolyn is watching this closely.

                    JANE
    (uncomfortable)
Well, what do you expect? You can't all
of a sudden be my best friend, just
because you had a bad day.

She gets up and heads toward the kitchen.

                    JANE
I mean, hello. You've barely even spoken
to me for months.

She's gone. Lester notices Carolyn looking at him critically.

                    LESTER
Oh, what, you're mother-of-the-year? You
treat her like an employee.

                                    (CONTINUED)

CONTINUED: (2)

                    CAROLYN
               (taken aback)
          What?!

Lester is quiet, staring at his plate.

                    CAROLYN
               (more authority)
          What?

Lester gets up and starts after Jane, taking his plate with
him.

                    LESTER
          I'm going to get some ice cream.

Carolyn watches him go, irritated.

INT. BURNHAM HOUSE - CONTINUOUS

Jane stands at the sink, rinsing off her plate. Lester
enters.

                    LESTER
          Honey, I'm sorry. I...

Jane turns and stares at him, waiting for him to finish.

                    LESTER
          I'm sorry I haven't been more available,
          I just... I'm...

He's looking to her for a little help here, but she's too
uncomfortable with this sudden intimacy to give him any.

                    LESTER
               (finally)
          You know, you don't always have to wait
          for me to come to you...

                    JANE
          Oh, great. So now it's my fault?

                    LESTER
          I didn't say that. It's nobody's fault.
          Janie, what happened? You and I used to
          be pals.

EXT. BURNHAM HOUSE - CONTINUOUS

On VIDEO: We're looking through GREENHOUSE WINDOWS at Lester
and Jane in the kitchen . We can't hear what they're saying,
but it's obvious it's not going well.

                                              (CONTINUED)

CONTINUED:

Jane puts her plate in the dishwasher and leaves. We FOLLOW HER out the door, then the camera JERKS back to Lester calling after her.

CLOSE on the face of RICKY FITTS, illuminated by the screen of his DIGICAM as he videotapes. Ricky is eighteen, but his eyes are much older. Beneath his Zen-like tranquility lurks something wounded... and dangerous.

His POV, **on VIDEO**: Through the kitchen window, we see Lester at the sink, rinsing off his plate, muttering to himself. His head suddenly jerks up and he looks at us, as if he realizes he's being watched.

INT. BURNHAM HOUSE - KITCHEN - CONTINUOUS

Lester's POV: We're looking out through the kitchen window at the point where Ricky was just standing, but he's no longer there.

Lester turns off the faucet, dries his hands, then tosses the towel on the counter on his way out, where it lands next to a framed PHOTOGRAPH of Lester, Carolyn, and a much-younger Jane, taken several years earlier at an amusement park.

It's startling how happy they look.

EXT. SALE HOUSE - DAY

CLOSE on a wooden SIGN that reads:

OPEN HOUSE TODAY
BURNHAM & ASSOCIATES REALTY
555-0195 Carolyn Burnham

The sign is planted in front of a RUN-DOWN HOME in a run-down neighborhood. The Mercedes is parked in front of the house. Carolyn, wearing a smart business suit, is unloading a box of cleaning supplies and a BOOMBOX from the back of the Mercedes when something across the street catches her eye.

Her POV: In front of a different house with much more curb appeal is another SIGN, featuring a picture of a handsome silver-haired MAN. It reads:

Another One SOLD By Buddy Kane
The Real Estate King 555-0100

Carolyn frowns and slams the back of the Mercedes shut.

INT. SALE HOUSE - LIVING ROOM - MOMENTS LATER

The interior of this house is ugly, oppressive and tasteless.
Carolyn opens the front door, breathes deeply and solemnly
announces:

                    CAROLYN
          I will sell this house today.

She neatly arranges her sales materials on a desk, then
strips down to her undergarments.

MONTAGE:

We see Carolyn, working with fierce concentration as she:

Cleans glass doors that overlook the patio and pool;

Doggedly scrubs countertops in the kitchen;

Perches on a stepladder to dust a cheap-looking ceiling fan
in the master bedroom;

And vacuums a dirty carpet that will never be clean.

Throughout all this, she keeps repeating to herself:

                    CAROLYN
          I will sell this house today.
          I will sell this house today.
          I will sell this house today.

INT. SALE HOUSE - BATHROOM - LATER

Carolyn stands in front of the mirror, wearing her suit once
more, applying lipstick. She stares at her reflection
critically.

                    CAROLYN
          I will sell this house today.

She says this as if it were a threat, then notices a smudge
on the mirror and wipes it off.

EXT. SALE HOUSE - FRONT YARD - LATER

The front door opens to reveal Carolyn, greeting us with the
smile she thinks could sell ice to an Eskimo.

                    CAROLYN
          Welcome. I'm Carolyn Burnham!

INT. SALE HOUSE - FOYER - CONTINUOUS

Smiling, Carolyn leads a man and woman into the living room.
They're thirtyish, and they've seen a lot of houses today.

>                    CAROLYN
>           This living room is very dramatic.
>           Wait 'til you see the native stone
>           fireplace!

The man and woman glance around the dark room, unimpressed.

>                    CAROLYN
>           A simple cream would really lighten
>           things up. You could even put in a
>           skylight.

The woman wrinkles her face, skeptical.

>                    CAROLYN
>           Well, why don't we go into the kitchen?

INT. SALE HOUSE - KITCHEN - LATER

Carolyn enters, followed by a different couple in their
fifties.

>                    CAROLYN
>           It's a dream come true for any cook. Just
>           filled with positive energy. Huh?

INT. SALE HOUSE - MASTER BEDROOM - LATER

Carolyn stands with a different couple: African American,
late twenties. The woman is pregnant.

>                    CAROLYN
>           ...and you'll be surprised how much a
>           ceiling fan can cut down on your energy
>           costs.

EXT. SALE HOUSE - BACK YARD - LATER

Carolyn stands by the pool next to two fortyish WOMEN.

>                    CAROLYN
>           You know, you could have some really fun
>           backyard get-togethers out here.

>                    WOMAN #1
>           The ad said this pool was "lagoon-like."
>           There's nothing "lagoon-like" about it.
>           Except for maybe the bugs.

(CONTINUED)

CONTINUED:

                    WOMAN #2
          There's not even any plants out here.

                    CAROLYN
               (re: shrub)
          What do you call this? Is this not a
          plant? If you have a problem with the
          plants, I can always call my landscape
          architect. Solved.

                    WOMAN #2
          I mean, I think "lagoon," I think
          waterfall, I think tropical. This is a
          cement hole.

A beat.

                    CAROLYN
          I have some tiki torches in the garage.

INT. SALE HOUSE - SUN ROOM - LATER

Carolyn enters, alone. She's furious. She locks the sliding
glass door and starts to pull the vertical blinds shut, then
stops. Standing very still, with the blinds casting shadows
across her face, she starts to cry: brief, staccato SOBS that
seemingly escape against her will. Suddenly she SLAPS
herself, hard.

                    CAROLYN
          Shut up. Stop it. You... Weak!

But the tears continue. She SLAPS herself again.

                    CAROLYN
          Weak. Baby. Shut up. Shut up! Shut up!

She SLAPS herself repeatedly until she stops crying. She
stands there, taking deep breaths until she has everything
under control, then pulls the blinds shut, once again all
business. She walks out calmly, leaving us alone in the dark,
empty room.

We HEAR CHEERING and APPLAUSE.

INT. HIGH SCHOOL GYMNASIUM - NIGHT

We're at a high-school BASKETBALL GAME. Teenage boys play a
fast and furious game. One team wearing pale blue and white
uniforms scores a basket. Perky cheerleaders jump up and down
as the CROWD goes wild.

                                        (CONTINUED)

CONTINUED:

Seated in the bleachers, next to the high school BAND, is a
group of about twenty TEENAGE GIRLS, dressed in pale blue and
white uniforms. Among them, Jane sits next to ANGELA HAYES.
At sixteen, Angela is strikingly beautiful; with perfect even
features, blonde hair and a nubile young body, she's the
archetypal American dream girl.

Jane stands and scans the bleachers.

                    ANGELA
          Who are you looking for?

                    JANE
          My parents are coming tonight. They're
          trying to, you know, take an active
          interest in me.

                    ANGELA
          Gross. I hate it when my mom does that.

                    JANE
          They're such assholes. Why can't they
          just have their own lives?

INT. MERCEDES-BENZ ML320 - CONTINUOUS

Carolyn drives. Lester is slumped in the passenger seat.

                    LESTER
          What makes you so sure she wants us to be
          there? Did she ask us to come?

                    CAROLYN
          Of course not. She doesn't want us to
          know how important this is to her. But
          she's been practicing her steps for
          weeks.

                    LESTER
          Well, I bet money she's going to resent
          it. And I'm missing the James Bond
          marathon on TNT.

                    CAROLYN
          Lester, this is important. I'm sensing a
          real distance growing between you and
          Jane.

                    LESTER
          Growing? She hates me.

                    CAROLYN
          She's just willful.

                                        (CONTINUED)

CONTINUED:

                        LESTER
          She hates you too.

Carolyn stares at him, unsure of how to respond.

INT. HIGH SCHOOL GYMNASIUM - LATER

The uniformed girls now stand in formation on the gym floor.

                     ANNOUNCER
          (over P.A.)
          And now, for your half-time
          entertainment, Rockwell High's award-
          winning Dancing Spartanettes!

In the crowded stands, Lester and Carolyn find seats.

                       LESTER
          We can leave right after this, right?

The HIGH SCHOOL BAND plays "ON BROADWAY." On the gym floor,
the girls perform . They're well-rehearsed, but too young to
carry off the ambitious Vegas routine they're attempting.

Lester, watching from the stands, picks out his daughter.

His POV: Jane performs well, concentrating. Dancing awkwardly
next to her is Angela. Suddenly Angela looks right at us and
smiles... a lazy, insolent smile.

Lester leans forward in his seat.

His POV: We're focused on Angela now. Everything starts to
SLOW DOWN... the MUSIC acquires an eerie ECHO...

We ZOOM slowly toward Lester as he watches, transfixed.

His POV: Angela's awkwardness gives way to a fluid grace, and
"ON BROADWAY" FADES into dreamy, hypnotic MUSIC. The light on
Angela grows stronger, and the other girls DISAPPEAR
entirely.

Lester is suddenly alone in the stands, spellbound.

His POV: Angela looks directly at us now, dancing only for
Lester. Her movements take on a blatantly erotic edge as she
starts to unzip her uniform, teasing us with an expression
that's both innocent and knowing, then... she pulls her
uniform OPEN and a profusion of RED ROSE PETALS spill
forth... and we SMASH CUT TO:

INT. HIGH SCHOOL GYMNASIUM - CONTINUOUS

Angela, fully clothed, is once again surrounded by the other girls. The HIGH SCHOOL BAND plays its last note, the Dancing Spartanettes strike their final pose, and the audience APPLAUDS.

Carolyn claps along with the rest of the audience. Lester just sits there, unable to take his eyes off Angela.

EXT. HIGH SCHOOL GYMNASIUM - LATER

The game is long over. Jane and Angela come out of the gym.

                    JANE
          Oh shit, they're still here.

Her POV: Lester and Carolyn stand at the edge of the parking lot.

                    LESTER
          Janie!

                    CAROLYN
          Hi! I really enjoyed that!

She crosses reluctantly toward her parents, followed by Angela.

                    LESTER
          Congratulations, honey, you were great.

                    JANE
          I didn't win anything.

                    LESTER
               (to Angela)
          Hi, I'm Lester. Janie's dad.

                    ANGELA
          Oh. Hi.

An awkward beat.

                    JANE
          This is my friend, Angela Hayes.

                    LESTER
          Okay, good to meet you. You were also
          good tonight. Very... precise.

CONTINUED:

                    ANGELA
          (warming)
     Thanks.

                    CAROLYN
          (to Angela)
     Nice to meet you, Angela.
          (to Jane)
     Honey, I'm so proud of you. I watched you
     very closely, and you didn't screw up
     once.
          (then, to Lester)
     Okay, we have to go.

She starts toward the parking lot. Lester stays behind.

                    LESTER
     So, what are you girls doing now?

                    JANE
     Dad.

                    ANGELA
     We're going out for pizza.

                    LESTER
     Oh really, do you need a ride? We can
     give you a ride. I have a car. You wanna
     come with us?

                    ANGELA
     Thanks... but I have a car.

                    LESTER
     Oh, you have a car. Oh. That's great!
     That's great, because Janie's thinking
     about getting a car soon too, aren't you,
     honey?

                    JANE
          (you freak)
     Dad. Mom's waiting for you.

                    LESTER
     Well, it was very nice meeting you,
     Angela. Any, uh, friend of Janie's is a
     friend of mine.

Angela smiles, aware of the power she has over him. He is
mesmerized; grateful, even.

                    LESTER
     Well... I'll be seeing you around then.

(CONTINUED)

CONTINUED: (2)

Lester waves awkwardly as he crosses off.

>                    JANE
>          Could he <u>be</u> any more pathetic?

>                    ANGELA
>          I think it's sweet. And I think he and
>          your mother have not had sex in a long
>          time.

## INT. BURNHAM HOUSE - MASTER BEDROOM - A FEW HOURS LATER

CLOSE on a solitary red ROSE PETAL as it falls slowly through
the air.

We're looking down on Lester and Carolyn in bed. Even in
sleep, Carolyn looks determined. Lester is awake and stares
up at us.

>                    LESTER (V.O.)
>          It's the weirdest thing.

The ROSE PETAL drifts into view, landing on his pillow.

>                    LESTER (V.O.)
>          I feel like I've been in a coma for about
>          twenty years, and I'm just now waking up.

More ROSE PETALS fall onto the bed, and he smiles up at...

His POV: Angela, naked, FLOATS above us as a deluge of ROSE
PETALS falls around her. Her hair fans out around her head
and GLOWS with a subtle, burnished light. She looks down at
us with a smile that is all things...

Lester smiles back and LAUGHS, as ROSE PETALS cover his face.

>                    LESTER (V.O.)
>          Spec-tac-ular.

## EXT. ROBIN HOOD TRAIL - CONTINUOUS

A WHITE BMW 328si CONVERTIBLE is parked on the street outside
the Burnham's house. We HEAR girlish LAUGHTER from inside.

## INT. ANGELA'S BMW - CONTINUOUS

Angela is behind the wheel, Jane in the passenger seat.
They're passing a JOINT back and forth.

>                    JANE
>          I'm sorry my dad was so weird tonight.

CONTINUED:

                     ANGELA
It's okay. I'm used to guys drooling over
me. It started when I was about twelve,
I'd go out to dinner with my parents.
Every Thursday night, Red Lobster. And
every guy there would stare at me when I
walked in. And I knew what they were
thinking. Just like I knew guys at school
thought about me when they jerked off.

                     JANE
Vomit.

                     ANGELA
No, I liked it. And I still like it. If
people I don't even know look at me and
want to fuck me, it means I really have a
shot at being a model. Which is great,
because there's nothing worse in life
than being ordinary.

An awkward beat. Jane stares at the floor.

                     JANE
I really think it'll happen for you.

                     ANGELA
Oh, I know. Because everything that was
meant to happen, does. Eventually.

EXT. BURNHAM HOUSE - CONTINUOUS

**On VIDEO:** Jane gets out of the car, still LAUGHING, and waves
as Angela pulls away. We ZOOM toward Jane as she walks up the
driveway. She turns suddenly, sensing our presence.

Her POV: We're looking at the COLONIAL HOUSE next door where
the moving van was parked earlier. The front porch is
shrouded in darkness... then a PORCH LIGHT abruptly reveals
Ricky. As usual, he's dressed conservatively. There is a
BEEPER attached to his belt, and his DIGICAM dangles loosely
around his neck.

Irritated, Jane stares at him, hard.

                     JANE
Asshole.

He looks back at her curiously, then raises his Digicam and
starts to videotape her.

His POV, **on VIDEO:** Jane, angry and self-conscious, turns and
walks quickly toward her house, flipping us off as she goes.

INT. BURNHAM HOUSE - FOYER - CONTINUOUS

Jane enters, closes and locks the door. She quickly TURNS OFF
THE LIGHT that's been left on for her, then peeks through a
window.

Her POV: There's no sign of Ricky.

Jane turns back into the room, her heart racing... and
smiles.

INT. BURNHAM HOUSE - JANE'S BEDROOM - THE NEXT MORNING

CLOSE on an ADDRESS BOOK: A man's hand flips to the H page
and then his finger stops at the name Angela Hayes.

Lester, dressed for work, goes through Jane's address book.
We HEAR the SHOWER running in the adjacent bathroom. He grabs
Jane's phone and dials, then stands with the receiver to his
ear, nervous.

                    ANGELA
               (over phone line)
          Hello? Hello?

Lester is frozen, unable to speak. Suddenly, the SHOWER is
turned off in the next room. Lester hangs up and exits
quickly. A moment, then the PHONE RINGS. Jane emerges from
the bathroom, a towel wrapped around her torso, drying her
wet hair. She picks up the PHONE.

                    JANE
          Hello?

INT. HAYES HOUSE - ANGELA'S BEDROOM - CONTINUOUS

Angela is sprawled across her bed, on the phone.

                    ANGELA
          Why'd you call me?

INTERCUT WITH JANE IN HER BEDROOM:

                    JANE
          I didn't.

                    ANGELA
          Well, my phone just rang and I answered
          it and somebody hung up and then I star
          sixty-nined and it called you back.

                    JANE
          I was in the shower.

                                        (CONTINUED)

CONTINUED:

Then Jane notices her address book open to the H page.

>                    JANE
>          Oh, gross.

EXT. BURNHAM HOUSE - CONTINUOUS

**On VIDEO:** We're across from Jane's WINDOW, looking in. Jane
picks up the address book, frowning. She speaks into the
phone, but we can't hear her.

>                WOMAN'S VOICE (O.C.)
>          (sing song)
>          Rick-y! Break-fast!

INT. FITTS HOUSE - RICKY'S BEDROOM - CONTINUOUS

Ricky stands at his window, videotaping. He lowers his
Digicam, but his eyes remain locked on Jane across the way.

>                    RICKY
>          Be right there.

INT. FITTS HOUSE - KITCHEN - MOMENTS LATER

BARBARA FITTS stands at the stove, flipping bacon strips
mechanically, her eyes focused elsewhere. At least ten years
younger than her husband, she's pretty in a June Cleaver-ish
way. The Colonel sits at a dinette reading The Wall Street
Journal. Ricky enters.

>                    RICKY
>     Mom.

Startled, Barbara turns to him.

>                    BARBARA
>          Hello.

As she attempts to serve him bacon:

>                    RICKY
>          I don't eat bacon, remember?

>                    BARBARA
>          (unnerved)
>          I'm sorry, I must have forgotten.

Ricky serves himself scrambled eggs from another pan, then
joins his father at the table.

>                    RICKY
>          What's new in the world, Dad?

CONTINUED:

                    COLONEL
        This country is going straight to hell.

A DOORBELL rings. The Colonel and Barbara look at each other,
alarmed.

                    COLONEL
        Are you expecting anyone?

                BARBARA
    No.
        (thinks)
    No.

The Colonel heads toward the living room, a little puffed up.

INT. FITTS HOUSE - FOYER - MOMENTS LATER

The Colonel opens the front door to reveal the two JIMS.

                JIM #1
    Hi.

                JIM #2
    Welcome to the neighborhood.

Jim #1 holds out a basket filled with flowers, vegetables and
a small white cardboard box tied with raffia.

                JIM #1
    Just a little something from our garden.

                JIM #2
    Except for the pasta, we got that at
    Fallaci's.

                JIM #1
    It's unbelievably fresh. You just drop it
    in the water and it's done.

The Colonel stares at them, suspicious.

                JIM #1
        (offers his hand)
    Jim Olmeyer. Two doors down. Welcome to
    the neighborhood.

                COLONEL
        (shakes)
    Colonel Frank Fitts, U.S. Marine Corps.

CONTINUED:

                    JIM #1
          Nice to meet you. And this is my
          partner...

                    JIM #2
               (offers his hand)
          Jim Berkley, but people call me J.B.

                    COLONEL
          Let's cut to the chase, okay? What are
          you guys selling?

                    JIM #2
               (after a beat)
          Nothing. We just wanted to say hi to our
          new neighbors--

                    COLONEL
          Yeah, yeah, yeah. But you said you're
          partners. So what's your business?

The Jims look at each other, then back at the Colonel.

                    JIM #1
          Well, he's a tax attorney.

                    JIM #2
          And he's an anesthesiologist.

The Colonel looks at them, confused. Then it dawns on him.

INT. COLONEL'S FORD EXPLORER - LATER

The Colonel drives, staring darkly at the road ahead. In the
passenger seat, Ricky is using a CALCULATOR and jotting
numbers down in a NOTEBOOK.

                    COLONEL
          How come these faggots always have to rub
          it in your face? How can they be so
          shameless?

                    RICKY
          That's the whole thing, Dad. They don't
          feel like it's anything to be ashamed of.

The Colonel looks at Ricky sharply.

                    COLONEL
          Well, it is.

A beat, as Ricky continues his calculations, before he
realizes a response is expected from him. Then:

CONTINUED:

                    RICKY
          Yeah, you're right.

The Colonel's eyes flash angrily.

                    COLONEL
          Don't placate me like I'm your mother,
          boy.

Ricky sighs, then looks at his father.

                    RICKY
          Forgive me, sir, for speaking so bluntly,
          but those fags make me want to puke my
          fucking guts out.

The Colonel is taken aback but quickly covers.

                    COLONEL
          Me too, son. Me too.

Case closed, Ricky goes back to his calculations.

CLOSE on the pencil in his hands: He's totaling two columns
of NUMBERS. Under the column "Income" he writes in swift,
bold strokes: $24,950.00.

EXT. HIGH SCHOOL CAMPUS - A SHORT TIME LATER

Jane and Angela are standing with two other TEENAGE GIRLS.

                    ANGELA
          I'm serious, he just pulled down his
          pants and yanked it out. You know, like,
          say hello to Mr. Happy.

                    TEENAGE GIRL #1
          Gross.

                    ANGELA
          It wasn't gross. It was kind of cool.

                    TEENAGE GIRL #1
          So, did you do it with him?

                    ANGELA
          Of course I did. He is a really well-
          known photographer? He shoots for Elle on
          like, a regular basis? It would have been
          so majorly stupid of me to turn him down.

                    TEENAGE GIRL #2
          You are a total prostitute.

CONTINUED:

                      ANGELA
       Hey. That's how things really are. You
       just don't know, because you're this
       pampered little suburban chick.

                 TEENAGE GIRL #2
       So are you. You've only been in _Seventeen_
       once, and you looked fat, so stop acting
       like you're goddamn Christy Turlington.

The two TEENAGE GIRLS move away from Jane and Angela.

                      ANGELA
         (calling off)
       Cunt!
         (then)
       I am so sick of people taking their
       insecurities out on me.

The Colonel's Ford Explorer pulls up, and Ricky gets out.

                      JANE
       Oh my God. That's the pervert who filmed
       me last night.

                      ANGELA
       Him? Jane. No way. He's a total lunatic.

                      JANE
       You know him?

                      ANGELA
       Yeah. We were on the same lunch shift
       when I was in ninth grade, and he would
       always say the most random, weird things,
       and then one day, he was just like, gone.
       And then, Connie Cardullo told me his
       parents had to put him in a mental
       institution.

                      JANE
       Why? What did he do?

                      ANGELA
       What do you mean?

                      JANE
       Well, they can't put you away just for
       saying weird things.

Angela stares at Jane, then her mouth widens into a smile.

ANGELA
You total slut. You've got a crush on
him.

JANE
What? Please.

ANGELA
You were defending him! You love him. You
want to have like, ten thousand of his
babies.

JANE
Shut up.

Jane suddenly finds Ricky standing in front of her.

RICKY
Hi. My name's Ricky. I just moved next
door to you.

JANE
I know. I kinda remember this really
creepy incident when you were filming me
last night?

RICKY
I didn't mean to scare you. I just think
you're interesting.

Angela shoots a wide-eyed look at Jane, who ignores it.

JANE
Thanks, but I really don't need to have
some psycho obsessing about me right now.

RICKY
I'm not obsessing. I'm just curious.

He looks at her intently, his eyes searching hers. Jane is
unnerved and has to look away. Ricky smiles and walks off.

ANGELA
What a freak. And why does he dress like
a Bible salesman?

JANE
He's like, so confident. That can't be
real.

ANGELA
I don't believe him. I mean, he didn't
even like, look at me once.

INT. FITTS HOUSE - DEN - THAT NIGHT

CLOSE on a TV SCREEN: "Hogan's Heroes" on Nick at Nite.

The Colonel and Barbara are seated on a couch, watching
television. The Colonel is smiling, enjoying the show;
Barbara just stares. The Colonel CHUCKLES at a joke and
startles her.

We HEAR a door opening elsewhere in the house, and Ricky
enters.

                    RICKY
          Hey.

He sits on the couch, next to his father, and watches TV
along with them. The Colonel's smile fades.

                    BARBARA
             (out of the blue)
          I'm sorry, what?

                    RICKY
          Mom. Nobody said anything.

                    BARBARA
          Oh. I'm sorry.

The three of them stare at the TV, like strangers in an
airport.

INT. HOTEL BALLROOM - NIGHT

We HEAR MUSIC under a room full of people all talking at
once, as Lester and Carolyn enter a hotel ballroom. We FOLLOW
THEM as they pass a SIGN that reads:

GREATER ROCKWELL REALTOR RESOURCES GROUP

                    CAROLYN
          --everyone here is with their spouse or
          their significant other. How would it
          look if I showed up with no one?

                    LESTER
          Well, you always end up ignoring me and
          going off--

Inside the ballroom, well-dressed real estate professionals
stand in clumps, chatting. Catering waiters serve hors
d'eouvres.

CONTINUED:

                    CAROLYN
          Now listen to me. This is an important
          business function. As you know, my
          business is selling an image. And part of
          my job is to <u>live</u> that image--

                    LESTER
          Just say whatever you want to say and
          spare me the propaganda.

                    CAROLYN
               (spots someone)
          Hi, Shirley!
               (to Lester)
          Listen, just do me a favor. Act happy
          tonight?

                    LESTER
               (grins stupidly)
          I <u>am</u> happy, honey.

Carolyn's jaw tightens, then:

                    CAROLYN
               (spots someone)
          Oh! Buddy!

She drags Lester toward a silver-haired MAN and his much
younger WIFE. We recognize the Man as BUDDY KANE, The Real
Estate King.

                    CAROLYN
               (shakes Buddy's hand)
          Buddy! Buddy. Hi! Good to see you again.

                    BUDDY
          It's so good to see you too, Catherine.

                    CAROLYN
          Carolyn.

                    BUDDY
          Carolyn! Of course. How are you?

                    CAROLYN
          Very well, thank you.
               (to his wife)
          Hello, Christy.

                    CHRISTY
          Hello.

CONTINUED: (2)

                    CAROLYN
          My husband, Lester--

                    BUDDY
               (shakes Lester's hand)
          It's a pleasure.

                    LESTER
          Oh, we've met before, actually. This
          thing last year. Or the Christmas thing
          at the Sheraton.

                    BUDDY
          Oh, yes.

                    LESTER
          It's okay. I wouldn't remember me either.

He LAUGHS. A little too loudly. Carolyn quickly joins in.

                    CAROLYN
               (forced gaiety)
          Honey. Don't be weird.

She smiles her most winning smile at him. He knows this
persona well, only it's never pissed him off as much as it
does right now.

                    LESTER
          All right, honey. I won't be weird.
               (his face close to hers)
          I'll be whatever you want me to be.

And he kisses her--a soft, warm kiss that speaks unmistakably
of sex--then turns to the others and grins.

                    LESTER
          We have a very healthy relationship.

                    BUDDY
          I see.

Carolyn's smile is frozen on her face.

                    LESTER
          Well. I don't know about you, but I need
          a drink.

He crosses off. Carolyn, Buddy and Christy watch him go.

INT. HOTEL BALLROOM - MOMENTS LATER

Lester stands at the bar. A bartender pours him a drink.

                                        (CONTINUED)

CONTINUED:

>                    LESTER
>          Whoa. Put a little more in there, cowboy.

The bartender complies. Lester takes his drink and turns to face the center of the room.

His POV: Carolyn is talking to Buddy and Christy. She's on: smiling, animated, LAUGHING too loud at their jokes.

Lester shakes his head. Ricky approaches him, wearing a waiter's uniform, carrying a tray of empty glasses.

>                    RICKY
>          Excuse me. Don't you live on Robin Hood
>          Trail? The house with the red door?

>                    LESTER
>              (suspicious)
>          Yeah.

>                    RICKY
>          I'm Ricky Fitts. I just moved into the
>          house next to you.

>                    LESTER
>          Oh. Hi, Ricky Fitts. I'm Lester Burnham.

>                    RICKY
>          Hi, Lester Burnham.

A beat. Lester looks away, scans the crowd, then downs the rest of his drink in one gulp. Ricky just stands there, watching him. Finally Lester turns back to Ricky: what does this kid want?

>                    RICKY (cont'd)
>          Do you party?

>                    LESTER
>          Excuse me?

>                    RICKY
>          Do you get high?

Lester's surprised, but instantly intrigued.

INT. HOTEL BALLROOM - MOMENTS LATER

Carolyn and Buddy are deep in conversation. Christy has wandered off. Carolyn is nervous; Buddy seems amused.

CONTINUED:

                  CAROLYN
You know, I probably wouldn't even tell
you this if I weren't a little tipsy,
but... I am in complete awe of you. I
mean, your firm is, hands down, the Rolls
Royce of local Real Estate firms, and
your personal sales record is, is, is
very intimidating. You know, I'd love to
sit down with you and just pick your
brain, if you'd ever be willing. I
suppose, technically, I'm the
"competition," but... I mean, hey, I
don't flatter myself that I'm even in the
same league as you...

                  BUDDY
I'd love to.

                  CAROLYN
   (shocked)
Really?

                  BUDDY
Absolutely. Call my secretary and have
her schedule a lunch.

                  CAROLYN
I'll do that. Thank you.

They look at each other for a beat, then look away. This
situation is loaded and they both know it.

EXT. HOTEL - LATER

Ricky and Lester stand next to a dumpster behind the service
entrance to the hotel, smoking a JOINT.

                  LESTER
...did you ever see that movie, where the
body's walking around holding its own
head? And then the head goes down on that
babe?

                  RICKY
Re-Animator.

Suddenly, the service entrance opens, and a large CATERING
BOSS in a cheap suit peers out at them. Ricky hides the
joint.

                CATERING BOSS
   (to Ricky)
Look. I'm not paying you to...
      (MORE)

(CONTINUED)

CONTINUED:

                            CATERING BOSS (cont'd)
                  (eyes Lester, suspiciously)
...do whatever it is you're doing out
here.

                            RICKY
Fine. So don't pay me.

                          CATERING BOSS
Excuse me?

                            RICKY
I quit. So you don't have to pay me. Now,
leave me alone.

                          CATERING BOSS
Asshole.

He goes back inside. Lester looks at Ricky, who shrugs.

                            LESTER
I think you just became my personal hero.
                  (then)
Doesn't that make you nervous, just
quitting your job like that? Well, I
guess when you're all of, what? Sixteen?

                            RICKY
Eighteen.
                  (then)
I just do these gigs as a cover. I have
other sources of income. But my dad
interferes less in my life when I pretend
to be an upstanding young citizen with a
respectable job.

                          CAROLYN (O.C.)
Lester?

Carolyn is standing in the open service entrance. Lester
quickly hides the joint behind his back.

                          CAROLYN
What are you doing?

                            LESTER
Honey, this is...
                  (laughs)
Ricky Fitts. This is Ricky Fitts.

                            RICKY
I'm Ricky Fitts, I just moved in the
house next to you. I go to school with
your daughter.

                         LESTER
              With Jane? Really?

                         RICKY
              Yeah. Jane.

                         CAROLYN
              Hi.
                   (then, to Lester)
              I'm ready to go. I'll meet you out front.

And she goes back inside.

                         LESTER
              Uh-oh. I'm in trouble. Nice meeting you,
              Ricky Fitts. Thanks for the, uh, thing.

                         RICKY
              Any time.

Lester goes inside.

                         RICKY
                   (calls after him)
              Lester. If you want any more, you know
              where I live.

INT. BURNHAM HOUSE - FAMILY ROOM - LATER

Jane and Angela are watching MTV. We HEAR the back door open.

                         JANE
              Oh, shit. They're home. Quick, let's go
              up to my room.

Jane switches off the TV.

                         ANGELA
              I should say hi to your dad.
                   (off Jane's look)
              I don't want to be rude.

She starts toward the kitchen. Jane doesn't like this.

INT. BURNHAM HOUSE - KITCHEN - CONTINUOUS

Lester enters and opens the refrigerator.

                         ANGELA (O.C.)
              Nice suit.

He turns, and is instantly transfixed by:

CONTINUED:


His POV: Angela leans against the counter, twirling her hair.

                    ANGELA
          You're looking good, Mr. Burnham.

She starts toward him.

                    ANGELA
          Last time I saw you, you looked kind of
          wound up.
               (spots something)
          Ooh, is that root beer?

She reaches inside the refrigerator to grab a bottle. As she
does, she moves to place her other hand casually on Lester's
shoulder. He sees it coming. Everything SLOWS DOWN, and all
sound FADES...

EXTREME CLOSE UP on her hand as it briefly touches his
shoulder in SLOW MOTION. We HEAR only the amplified BRUSH of
her fingers against the fabric of his suit, and its
unnatural, hollow ECHO...

BACK IN REAL TIME: She grabs the root beer and smiles at him.

CLOSE on Lester: his eyes narrow slightly, then:

He cups her face in his hands and kisses her. She seems
shocked, but doesn't resist as he pulls her toward him with
surprising strength. He breaks the kiss, looking at her in
awe, then he reaches up and touches his lips. His eyes widen
as he pulls a ROSE PETAL from his mouth right before we SMASH
CUT TO:

INT. BURNHAM HOUSE - KITCHEN - CONTINUOUS

Angela is back against the counter, drinking the root beer.
Lester stands by the refrigerator, gazing at her, still lost
in fantasy.

                    ANGELA
          I love root beer, don't you?

Jane watches from the doorway to the family room, feeling
incredibly awkward in her own home. Carolyn enters from the
dining room. Lester snaps out of it and grabs a root beer
from the refrigerator.

                    JANE
          Mom, you remember Angela.

                                              (CONTINUED)

CONTINUED:

                        CAROLYN
                  (her sales smile)
            Yes, of course!

                        JANE
            I forgot to tell you, she's spending the
            night. Is that okay?

                        LESTER
            Sure!

He takes a sip of his root beer, but it goes down the wrong
way and he starts COUGHING violently.

INT. BURNHAM HOUSE - JANE'S BEDROOM - LATER THAT NIGHT

Angela lays on the bed, in bra and panties, reading a
magazine. Jane, in an oversized T shirt, plays a video game
on her computer.

                        JANE
            I'm sorry about my dad.

                        ANGELA
            Don't be. I think it's funny.

                        JANE
            Yeah, to you, he's just another guy who
            wants to jump your bones. But to me...
            he's just too embarrassing to live.

                        ANGELA
            Your mom's the one who's embarrassing.
            What a phony.

Jane glances at Angela, irritated.

                        ANGELA
            Your dad's actually kind of cute.

                        JANE
            Shut up.

INT. BURNHAM HOUSE - HALLWAY - CONTINUOUS

Lester, still in his suit, stands outside Jane's room, his
ear up against the door. He can't believe what he's hearing.

                   ANGELA (O.C.)
            He is. If he just worked out a little,
            he'd be hot.

INT. BURNHAM HOUSE - JANE'S ROOM - CONTINUOUS

                    JANE
      Shut up.

                    ANGELA
      Oh, come on. Like you've never sneaked a
      peek at him in his underwear? I bet he's
      got a big dick.

                    JANE
      You are so grossing me out right now.

                    ANGELA
        (really enjoying this)
      If he built up his chest and arms, I
      would totally fuck him.

Jane covers her ears and starts SINGING to drown her out.

INT. BURNHAM HOUSE - HALLWAY - CONTINUOUS

Lester, still listening, looks like he's about to implode.

                  ANGELA (O.C.)
        (laughs)
      I would! I would suck your dad's big fat
      dick, and then I would fuck him 'til his
      eyes rolled back in his head!
        (then)
      What was that noise? Jane.

Jane's SINGING stops.

                  ANGELA (O.C.)
      I swear I heard something.

Panicked, Lester scurries down the hall.

INT. BURNHAM HOUSE - JANE'S BEDROOM - CONTINUOUS

                    JANE
      Yeah, it was the sound of you being a
      huge disgusting pig.

                    ANGELA
      I'm serious.

We HEAR the sharp TAP of a penny being thrown against glass.

                    ANGELA
      See?

(CONTINUED)

CONTINUED:


Angela crosses to the window and looks out.

>                    ANGELA
>               (spots something)
>          Oh my God. Jane.

EXT. BURNHAM HOUSE - CONTINUOUS

We see Angela standing at the window in her underwear,
looking down at us. Jane joins her and is immediately
unnerved by:

Their POV: In the Burnham's DRIVEWAY, the word "JANE" is
spelled out in FIRE.

INT. BURNHAM HOUSE - JANE'S BEDROOM - CONTINUOUS

>                    ANGELA
>          It's that psycho next door. Jane, what if
>          he worships you? What if he's got a
>          shrine with pictures of you surrounded by
>          dead people's heads and stuff?

>                    JANE
>          Shit. I bet he's filming us right now.

>                    ANGELA
>               (intrigued)
>          Really?

EXT. BURNHAM HOUSE - CONTINUOUS

**On VIDEO:** We're across from Jane's window, looking in. Jane
tries to shut the drapes, but Angela won't let her.
Irritated, Jane retreats into the room. We ZOOM toward her,
even as Angela poses in the window; we're clearly not
interested in Angela. The ZOOM continues, searching for Jane,
who has disappeared. Finally, we settle on the small make-up
MIRROR where we see a REFLECTION of Jane, back at her
computer. She's smiling. Then suddenly the DRAPES CLOSE and
she's gone.

INT. FITTS HOUSE - RICKY'S BEDROOM - CONTINUOUS

Ricky sits in darkness with his DIGICAM, videotaping. He
lowers the camera and smiles... then something below catches
his attention. He leans out the window to get a better look
at:

EXT. BURNHAM HOUSE - GARAGE - CONTINUOUS

Ricky's POV: Through a WINDOW on the side of the Burnham's GARAGE DOOR, we see Lester, still in his suit, digging through shelves against the back wall.

INT. BURNHAM HOUSE - GARAGE - CONTINUOUS

Lester digs through stuff stored on the shelves, searching for something as if his very life depended on it.

                    LESTER
          Shit. Shit!

He yanks aside COLLEGE YEARBOOKS, a racquetball RACQUET, boxes of old HOT ROD MAGAZINES, an unopened remote-controlled MODEL JEEP KIT, stacks of old vinyl LPs... finally his face lights up when he finds:

A pair of DUMBBELLS obviously unused for many years.

Lester rips off his jacket and tie and unbuttons his shirt. He glances around, finding his REFLECTION in the WINDOW as he pulls off his shirt, then the T-shirt underneath. He eyes himself critically: Angela was right, he's not in bad shape. Just a few extra pounds around his middle that wouldn't be hard to shed. He kicks off his shoes and begins to step out of his pants.

INT. FITTS HOUSE - RICKY'S BEDROOM - CONTINUOUS

Ricky holds his Digicam up and starts to videotape.

EXT. BURNHAM HOUSE - GARAGE - CONTINUOUS

Ricky's POV, **on VIDEO**: Through a WINDOW on the side of the Burnham's garage, we see Lester step out of his pants and briefs. Then, naked except for his black socks, he grabs the dumbbells and starts lifting them, watching his reflection in the window as he does.

INT. FITTS HOUSE - RICKY'S BEDROOM - CONTINUOUS

Ricky stands at the window, videotaping.

                    RICKY
          Welcome to America's Weirdest Home
          Videos.

Suddenly we HEAR someone trying to open a locked door.

                    COLONEL (O.C.)
          Ricky!

                                        (CONTINUED)

CONTINUED:


Moving swiftly, Ricky pulls the drapes shut and switches on a
light. His room is a haven of high-tech. A state-of-the-art
multimedia COMPUTER crowds his desk, and high-end STEREO and
VIDEO EQUIPMENT line the shelves, as well as HUNDREDS OF CDs.
There is easily twenty thousand dollars worth of equipment in
this room.

                    RICKY
          Coming, Dad.

                    COLONEL (O.C.)
          You know I don't like locked doors in my
          house, boy.

Ricky opens the door. The Colonel stands outside, eyeing him.

                    RICKY
          I'm sorry, I must have locked it by
          accident. So what's up?

The Colonel holds out a small PLASTIC CUP WITH A CAP.

                    COLONEL
          I need a urine sample.

                    RICKY
          Wow. It's been six months already. Can I
          give it to you in the morning? I just
          took a whiz.

                    COLONEL
          Yeah, I suppose.
               (an awkward beat)
          Well. Good night, son.

He disappears down the hall. Ricky smiles, shuts and locks
his door. He puts the plastic cup on the shelf, then crosses
to a MINI REFRIGERATOR in the corner of his room and takes
out a cup-sized TUPPERWARE CONTAINER from the freezer,
already filled with urine, albeit frozen, and places it on a
saucer to thaw overnight.

INT. BURNHAM HOUSE - MASTER BEDROOM - LATER THAT NIGHT

Carolyn lies sleeping. Lester is awake, staring at the
ceiling. After a moment, he gets up, taking care not to
disturb Carolyn, and walks toward the bathroom.

INT. BURNHAM HOUSE - MASTER BATH - CONTINUOUS

Lester enters and switches on the LIGHT. The room is filled
with STEAM. Lester looks around, confused, then focuses on:

                                             (CONTINUED)

CONTINUED:

His POV: Across from us, in a PEDESTAL BATHTUB, is Angela.
She smiles and beckons us, and we MOVE CLOSER. ROSE PETALS
float on the surface of the water, obscuring her naked body.

                    ANGELA
          I've been waiting for you.

Lester kneels by the bathtub like a man in church.

                    ANGELA
          You've been working out, haven't you? I
          can tell.

She arches her back and looks up at him provocatively.

                    ANGELA
          I was hoping you'd give me a bath... I'm
          very, very dirty.

Lester gives her a hard look, then slowly slips his hand into
the water between her legs. Her eyes widen and she throws her
head back... and we SMASH CUT TO:

INT. BURNHAM HOUSE - MASTER BEDROOM - CONTINUOUS

CLOSE on Carolyn, her eyes wide, listening to the rhythmic
BRUSH of Lester's hand as he masturbates under the covers.

She flips over and faces him.

                    CAROLYN
          What are you doing?

A beat.

                    LESTER
          Nothing.

Carolyn switches on the bedside LIGHT.

                    CAROLYN
          You were masturbating.

                    LESTER
          I was not.

                    CAROLYN
          Yes, you were.

He turns to her, trying to look innocent, then gives up.

                                             (CONTINUED)

CONTINUED:

> LESTER
> All right, so shoot me. I was whacking
> off.

Carolyn gets out of bed, repelled. Lester LAUGHS.

> LESTER
> That's right. I was choking the bishop.
> Shaving the carrot. Saying hi to my
> monster.

> CAROLYN
> That's disgusting.

> LESTER
> Well, excuse me, but I still have <u>blood</u>
> pumping through my veins!

> CAROLYN
> So do I!

> LESTER
> Really? I'm the only one who seems to be
> doing anything about it.

> CAROLYN
> Lester. I refuse to live like this. This
> is not a marriage.

> LESTER
> This hasn't been a marriage for years.
> But you were happy as long as I kept my
> mouth shut. Well, guess what? I've
> changed. And the new me whacks off when
> he feels horny, because you're obviously
> not going to help me out in that
> department.

> CAROLYN
> Oh. I see. You think you're the only one
> who's sexually frustrated?

> LESTER
> I'm not? Well then, come on, baby! I'm
> ready.

> CAROLYN
> (furious)
> Do not mess with me, mister, or I will
> divorce you so fast it'll make your head
> spin!

(CONTINUED)

CONTINUED: (2)

>                    LESTER
>          On what grounds? I'm not a drunk, I don't
>          fuck other women, I don't mistreat you,
>          I've never hit you, or even tried to
>          touch you since you made it so abundantly
>          clear just how unnecessary you consider
>          me to be. But. I did support you while
>          you got your license. And some people
>          might think that entitles me to half of
>          what's yours.

She sinks into a chair, stunned. It's clear he knows where
she's most vulnerable. He sees this, and likes it; it feels
good to win for a change. He curls up under the covers
contentedly.

>                    LESTER
>          Turn out the light when you come to bed,
>          okay?

CLOSE on Lester, smiling.

EXT. ROBIN HOOD TRAIL - EARLY MORNING

We're FLYING high above the neighborhood. Below us we see the
two Jims, jogging. We APPROACH them steadily.

>                    LESTER
>          It's a great thing when you realize you
>          still have the ability to surprise
>          yourself. Makes you wonder what else you
>          can do that you've forgotten about.

EXT. ROBIN HOOD TRAIL - CONTINUOUS

We're now at street level, FOLLOWING the two Jims.

>                    LESTER
>          Hey! You guys!

Still running, the Jims turn back in perfect unison, as
Lester runs INTO FRAME, wearing a baggy sweatshirt and a pair
of faded old sweatpants. The Jims slow down until he catches
up, then the three men run together in the early morning
light.

>                    JIM #2
>          Lester, I didn't know you ran.

>                    LESTER
>             (panting)
>          Well, I just started.

CONTINUED:

> JIM #1
> Good for you.

> LESTER
> I figured you guys might be able to give
> me some pointers. I need to shape up.
> Fast.

> JIM #1
> Well, are you just looking to lose
> weight, or do you want to have increased
> strength and flexibility as well?

> LESTER
> I want to look good naked.

EXT. FITTS HOUSE - A SHORT TIME LATER

The Colonel is washing his Ford Explorer, squatting to scrub
the bumper, when something catches his eye:

His POV: Lester and the Jims jog down the street.

The Colonel stands, scowling, as Ricky comes out of the
house, holding the URINE SAMPLE in front of him.

> COLONEL
> What is this, the fucking gay pride
> parade?

Lester breaks off from the two Jims and jogs up to Ricky and
the Colonel, out of breath. He grabs hold of his knees and
bends over, panting.

> LESTER
> Hey! Yo! Ricky!
> (re: the Jims)
> My entire life is passing before my eyes,
> and those two have barely broken a sweat.

He LAUGHS, and extends his hand to the Colonel.

> LESTER (cont'd)
> Sorry, hi. Lester Burnham, I live next
> door. We haven't met.

> COLONEL
> (shakes)
> Colonel Frank Fitts, U.S. Marine Corps.

> LESTER
> Whoa. Welcome to the neighborhood, sir.

CONTINUED:


He salutes the Colonel good-naturedly, grinning. The Colonel
doesn't think it's funny. An awkward beat.

>                    LESTER
>          So, Ricky, uh, I was thinking about the,
>          uh... I was gonna... the movie we talked
>          about...

>                    RICKY
>               (quickly)
>          Re-Animator.

>                    LESTER
>          Yeah!

>                    RICKY
>          You want to borrow it?
>               (before Lester can answer)
>          Okay, it's up in my room. Come on.

He heads into the house. Lester waves at the Colonel, then
follows him. The Colonel watches them go, his eyes dark.

INT. FITTS HOUSE - RICKY'S BEDROOM - MOMENTS LATER

Ricky enters, followed by Lester.

>                    RICKY
>          Can you hold this for a sec?

>                    LESTER
>          Sure.

He gives the URINE SPECIMEN to Lester, then locks the door.

>                    RICKY
>          I don't think my dad would try to come in
>          when somebody else is here, but you never
>          know.

Ricky crosses to a bureau and opens a DRAWER. He takes
clothing out and piles it on his bed.

>                    LESTER
>               (re: urine sample)
>          What is this?

>                    RICKY
>          Urine. I have to take a drug test every
>          six months to make sure I'm clean.

CONTINUED:

              LESTER
Are you kidding? You just smoked with me
last night.

              RICKY
It's not mine. One of my clients is a
nurse in a pediatrician's office. I cut
her a deal, she keeps me in clean piss.

Lester picks up a CD case from a shelf and examines it.

              LESTER
You like Pink Floyd?

              RICKY
I like a lot of music.

              LESTER
Man, I haven't listened to this album in
years.

He shakes his head, then puts the CD case down. Ricky, having
emptied the drawer, now removes a FALSE BOTTOM, revealing
rows of MARIJUANA, tightly packed in ZIP-LOC BAGS.

              RICKY
How much do you want?

              LESTER
I don't know, it's been a while. How much
is an ounce?

              RICKY
            (indicates bag)
Well, this is totally decent, and it's
three hundred.

              LESTER
Wow.

              RICKY
            (indicates another bag)
But this shit is top of the line. It's
called G-13. Genetically engineered by
the U.S. Government. Extremely potent.
But a completely mellow high, no
paranoia.

              LESTER
Is that what we smoked last night?

              RICKY
This is all I ever smoke.

                           (CONTINUED)

CONTINUED: (2)

                    LESTER
How much?

                    RICKY
Two grand.

                    LESTER
Jesus. Things have changed since 1973.

                    RICKY
You don't have to pay now. I know you're
good for it.

A beat.

                    LESTER
Thanks.

                    RICKY
              (hands him a bag)
There's a card in there with my beeper
number, call me anytime day or night. And
I only accept cash.

                    LESTER
              (looks around room)
Well, now I know how you can afford all
this equipment. When I was your age, I
flipped burgers all summer just to be
able to buy an eight track.

                    RICKY
That sucks.

                    LESTER
No actually, it was great. All I did was
party and get laid.
              (smiles)
I had my whole life ahead of me...

                    RICKY
My dad thinks I pay for all this with
catering jobs.
              (off Lester's look)
Never underestimate the power of denial.

Lester smiles. This kid's cool.

EXT. BURNHAM HOUSE - LATER

Carolyn, carrying a basket of fresh cut ROSES, passes by the
GARAGE WINDOW. From inside the garage, we HEAR ROCK MUSIC.

CONTINUED:

Carolyn stops and SNIFFS the air, frowning. She peers through the window.

Her POV: Lester, in a T-shirt and gym shorts, lies on a new WEIGHT BENCH, doing bench presses with shiny new BARBELLS.

INT. GARAGE - CONTINUOUS

ROCK MUSIC blasts from a new BOOMBOX on the floor.

The garage is in the process of becoming Lester's sanctuary. An ugly but comfortable 70's BOWL CHAIR has been pulled out and cleaned off, his old hot rod magazines strewn across it, and the remote-controlled MODEL JEEP KIT is spread across a card table. The SHELVES that Lester tore through earlier have been dismantled, leaving a blank wall on which now hangs a DART BOARD.

Lester finishes his last rep, straining, then puts the weights in their rack and sits up. As he takes a drag off a joint, the GARAGE DOOR suddenly starts to open. Lester looks up, squinting at:

His POV: The door raises to reveal Carolyn, silhouetted against the bright sunlight outside, pointing a REMOTE at us.

                    LESTER
          Uh-oh, mom's mad.

                    CAROLYN
          What the hell do you think you're doing?

                    LESTER
          Bench presses. I'm going to wail on my
          pecs, and then I'm going to do my back.

                    CAROLYN
          I see you're smoking pot now. I'm so
          glad. I think using illegal psychotropic
          substances is a very positive example to
          set for our daughter.

                    LESTER
          You're one to talk, you bloodless, money-
          grubbing freak.

                    CAROLYN
               (hostile)
          Lester. You have such hostility in you!

                    LESTER
          Do you mind? I'm trying to work out here.
               (then, suggestively)
          Unless you want to spot me.

                                        (CONTINUED)

CONTINUED:

                    CAROLYN
You will not get away with this. You can
be sure of that!

And she's gone. Lester leans back on the bench and grabs the
weights.

                    LESTER
         (as he lifts)
That's. What. You. Think.

INT. BRAD'S OFFICE - DAY

Brad is seated behind his desk, reading a document. Lester
sits across from him, smiling.

                    BRAD
         (reads)
"...my job consists of basically masking
my contempt for the assholes in charge,
and, at least once a day, retiring to the
men's room so I can jerk off, while I
fantasize about a life that doesn't so
closely resemble hell."
         (looks up at Lester)
Well, you obviously have no interest in
saving yourself.

                    LESTER
         (laughs)
Brad, for fourteen years I've been a
whore for the advertising industry. The
only way I could save myself now is if I
start firebombing.

                    BRAD
Whatever. Management wants you gone by
the end of the day.

                    LESTER
Well, just what sort of severance package
is "management" prepared to offer me?
Considering the information I have about
our editorial director buying pussy with
company money.

A beat.

                    LESTER (cont'd)
Which I'm sure would interest the I.R.S.,
since it technically constitutes fraud.
         (MORE)

CONTINUED:

> > LESTER (cont'd)
> > And I'm sure that some of our advertisers
> > and rival publications might like to know
> > about it as well. Not to mention, Craig's
> > wife.

Brad sighs.

> > BRAD
> > What do you want?

> > LESTER
> > One year's salary, with benefits.

> > BRAD
> > That's not going to happen.

> > LESTER
> > Well, what do you say I throw in a little
> > sexual harassment charge to boot?

Brad LAUGHS.

> > BRAD
> > Against who?

> > LESTER
> > Against you.

Brad stops laughing.

> > LESTER (cont'd)
> > Can you prove you didn't offer to save my
> > job if I'd let you blow me?

Brad leans back in his chair, studying Lester.

> > BRAD
> > Man. You are one twisted fuck.

> > LESTER
> > (standing)
> > Nope. I'm just an ordinary guy with
> > nothing to lose.

INT. OFFICE BUILDING - MOMENTS LATER

Exhilarated, Lester walks down a corridor, his belongings in
a box on his shoulder. He's happier than he's been in years.

> > LESTER
> > Yeah!

INT. RESTAURANT - LATER THAT DAY

Carolyn sits at a table, lost in thought. There are two menus
on the table. After a moment, Buddy Kane, the Real Estate
King, joins her. Carolyn immediately becomes warm and
gracious.

                    BUDDY
    Carolyn.

                    CAROLYN
    Buddy.

Carolyn smiles, genuinely touched that he remembers her name.

                    BUDDY
    I'm so sorry I kept you waiting. Christy
    left for New York this morning, and...
    let's just say things were very hectic
    around the house.

                    CAROLYN
    What's she doing in New York?

                    BUDDY
    She's moving there.
       (off Carolyn's look)
    Yes. We are splitting up.

                    CAROLYN
    Buddy. I'm so sorry.

                    BUDDY
       (bitterly)
    Yes, according to her, I'm too focused on
    my career. As if being driven to succeed
    is some sort of character flaw. Well, she
    certainly knew how to take advantage of
    the lifestyle my success afforded her.
    Oh. Wow.
       (then, laughing)
    Ah, it's for the best.

                    CAROLYN
    When I saw you two at the party the other
    night, you seemed perfectly happy.

                    BUDDY
    Well, call me crazy, but it is my
    philosophy that in order to be
    successful, one must project an image of
    success, at all times.

                                  (CONTINUED)

CONTINUED:


He smiles, then opens his menu. Carolyn picks hers up
mechanically, but continues to stare at him, enraptured, like
a fervent Christian who's just come face to face with Jesus.

EXT. HIGH SCHOOL CAMPUS - LATER THAT DAY

Ricky stands with his DIGICAM, videotaping something on the
ground at his feet.

**On VIDEO:** A DEAD BIRD lays on the ground, decomposing.

                    ANGELA (O.C.)
          What are you doing?

**On VIDEO:** The camera JERKS up to discover Jane and Angela
staring at us.

                    RICKY (O.C.)
          I was filming this dead bird.

                    ANGELA
          Why?

                    RICKY (O.C.)
          Because it's beautiful.

**On VIDEO:** Angela looks at Jane, trying not to laugh.

                    ANGELA
          I think maybe you forgot your medication
          today, mental boy.

**On VIDEO:** She falls out of frame as we ZOOM toward Jane.

                    RICKY (O.C.)
          Hi, Jane.

                    JANE
              (uncomfortable)
          Look. I want you to stop filming me.

Ricky lowers the Digicam.

                    RICKY
          Okay.

He looks at her, curious, his eyes searching hers. She
doesn't look away.

                    ANGELA
          Well, whatever.
              (to Jane)
          This is boring. Let's go.

CONTINUED:

> JANE
> (to Ricky)
> Do you need a ride?

> ANGELA
> (to Jane)
> Are you crazy? I don't want to end up
> hacked to pieces in a dumpster somewhere.

> RICKY
> It's okay. I'll walk. But thanks.

> ANGELA
> Yeah, see? He doesn't want to go anyway.
> C'mon, let's go.

Angela starts off, but Jane doesn't follow. Ricky smiles at
her. She almost smiles back, then:

> JANE
> (calls off to Angela)
> I think I'm going to walk, too.

Angela stops and stares at her.

> ANGELA
> What? Jane, that's like, almost a <u>mile</u>.

<u>EXT. TOP HAT MOTEL - LATER THAT DAY</u>

Carolyn's Mercedes is parked next to a JAGUAR CONVERTIBLE
with a VANITY LICENSE PLATE that reads "R E KING."

<u>INT. TOP HAT MOTEL - CONTINUOUS</u>

Carolyn and Buddy are in the middle of sex.

> CAROLYN
> Yes! Oh, God! I love it!

> BUDDY
> You like getting nailed by the king?

> CAROLYN
> Oh yes! I love it! Fuck me, your majesty!

<u>EXT. STREET - LATER THAT DAY</u>

Lester's TOYOTA CAMRY cruises through the streets. We hear
Lester SINGING along to "AMERICAN WOMAN" on the STEREO.

INT. TOYOTA CAMRY - CONTINUOUS

Lester is driving, smoking a joint.

> LESTER
> AMERICAN WOMAN, STAY AWAY FROM ME...
> AMERICAN WOMAN, MAMA LET ME BE... DON'T
> COME A HANGIN' AROUND MY DOOR... I DON'T
> WANT TO SEE YOUR FACE NO MORE...

EXT. MR. SMILEY'S - CONTINUOUS

Lester continues singing along to "AMERICAN WOMAN," as the Camry pulls into the parking lot of a FAST FOOD RESTAURANT.

Lester pulls up to the drive-thru speaker box.

> DRIVE-THRU GIRL (O.C.)
> (over speaker box)
> Smile you're at Mr. Smiley's.

Lester turns down the volume on the stereo.

> LESTER
> What?

> DRIVE-THRU GIRL (O.C.)
> Would you like to try our new bacon and
> egg fajita just a dollar twenty-nine for
> a limited time only.

> LESTER
> Uh... no. But thank you.
> (reading menu)
> I'll have a Big Barn Burger, Smiley
> fries, and an orange soda.

> DRIVE-THRU GIRL (O.C.)
> Please drive up to the window, thank you.

He pulls the car around to the WINDOW, where a teenage GIRL wearing a headset is waiting.

> DRIVE-THRU GIRL (cont'd)
> Smile, you're at Mr. Smiley's, that'll be
> four eighty-nine, please.

Lester pays her. As she hands him his food, he notices a SIGN in the corner of the window that reads:

NOW TAKING APPLICATIONS

(CONTINUED)

CONTINUED:

                      COUNTER GIRL
        Would you like some Smiley Sauce?

                      LESTER
        No. No, actually... I'd like to fill out
        an application.

She stares at him, confused by his age and attire.

                      COUNTER GIRL
        There's not jobs for manager, it's just
        for counter.

                      LESTER
        Good. I'm looking for the least possible
        amount of responsibility.

INT. MR. SMILEY'S - A SHORT TIME LATER

Lester sits at a booth with the MANAGER, a greasy kid wearing
a white short sleeve shirt and a tie covered with the Mr.
Smiley's logo. He looks over Lester's application, baffled.

                      MANAGER
        I don't think you'd fit in here.

                      LESTER
        I have fast food experience.

                      MANAGER
        Yeah, like twenty years ago.

                      LESTER
        Well, I'm sure there have been amazing
        technological advances in the industry,
        but surely you have some sort of training
        process. It seems unfair to presume I
        won't be able to learn.

The Manager sighs and runs a hand through his greasy hair,
wondering what he could possibly have done to deserve this.

INT. TOP HAT MOTEL - LATER THAT DAY

Carolyn and Buddy are in bed, post-sex.

                      CAROLYN
        That was exactly what I needed. The royal
        treatment, so to speak.

They laugh.

(CONTINUED)

CONTINUED:

                    CAROLYN
          I was <u>so</u> stressed out.

                    BUDDY
          Know what I do when I feel like that?

                    CAROLYN
          What?

                    BUDDY
          I fire a gun.

Carolyn sits up, eager to learn from the master.

                    CAROLYN
               (intrigued)
          Really.

                    BUDDY
          Oh yeah, I go to this little firing range
          downtown, and I just pop off a few
          rounds.

                    CAROLYN
               (embarrassed)
          I've never fired a gun before.

                    BUDDY
          Oh, you've gotta try it. Nothing makes
          you feel more powerful.
               (smiles seductively)
          Well, almost nothing.

Carolyn is quick to pick up her cue and kisses him, ready for
another round.

<u>EXT. SUBURBAN STREET - LATER THAT DAY</u>

Ricky and Jane walk along without speaking. He seems
comfortable with the silence; she doesn't. After a beat:

                    JANE
          So how do you like your new house?

                    RICKY
          I like it.

A beat.

CONTINUED:

                    JANE
The people who used to live there fed
these stray cats, so they were always
around, and it drove my mother nuts. And
then she cut down their tree.

An automobile FUNERAL PROCESSION appears and begins to pass
them slowly.

                    RICKY
Have you ever known anybody who died?

                    JANE
No.
      (a beat)
Have you?

                    RICKY
No, but I did see this homeless woman who
froze to death once. Just laying there on
the sidewalk. She looked really sad.

They watch the FUNERAL CARS pass.

                    RICKY
I got that homeless woman on video.

                    JANE
Why would you film that?

                    RICKY
Because it was amazing.

                    JANE
What was amazing about it?

A beat.

                    RICKY
When you see something like that, it's
like God is looking right at you, just
for a second. And if you're careful, you
can look right back.

                    JANE
And what do you see?

                    RICKY
Beauty.

INT. FITTS HOUSE - KITCHEN - MOMENTS LATER

Barbara Fitts sits at the kitchen table, staring off into space as if hypnotized. Behind her, Ricky enters, followed by Jane.

>                    RICKY
>          Mom, I want you to meet somebody.
>               (no response)
>          Mom.

Barbara's eyes flutter and she turns to him slowly.

>                    BARBARA
>               (pleasant)
>          Yes?

>                    RICKY
>          I want you to meet somebody. This is
>          Jane.

>                    JANE
>          Hi.

>                    BARBARA
>          Oh, my. I apologize for the way things
>          look around here.

Jane glances around. The room is spotless.

INT. FITTS HOUSE - THE COLONEL'S STUDY - MOMENTS LATER

We HEAR KEYS TURNING in the lock, then the door opens and Ricky enters, holding a RING OF KEYS, followed by Jane.

>                    RICKY
>          This is where my dad hides out.

GLASS CASES filled with GUNS line the walls.

>                    JANE
>          I take it he's got a thing for guns.

Ricky crosses to a built-in CABINET behind the desk.

>                    RICKY
>          You got to see this one thing...

He unlocks the cabinet and opens it, revealing shelves stacked with WAR MEMORABILIA.

(CONTINUED)

CONTINUED:

                    RICKY
          My dad would kill me if he knew I was in
          here.

                    JANE
          Did you steal his keys?

                    RICKY
          No. One of my clients is a locksmith. He
          was short on cash one night, so I let him
          pay me in trade.

He reaches into the cabinet and carefully removes an oval
CHINA PLATTER, which he hands to Jane. She examines it.

                    RICKY
          Turn it over.

CLOSE on the bottom of the plate: A small SWASTIKA is
imprinted in the center.

                    JANE
          Oh my God.

                    RICKY
          It's like official state china of the
          Third Reich. There's a whole subculture
          of people who collect this Nazi shit. But
          my dad just has this one thing.

He puts the platter back into the cabinet and shuts the door,
then notices Jane looking at him oddly.

                    RICKY
          What's wrong?

                    JANE
          Nothing.

                    RICKY
              (concerned)
          No, you're scared of me.

                    JANE
          No I'm not.

But she is. Ricky studies her.

                    RICKY
          You want to see the most beautiful thing
          I've ever filmed?

INT. FITTS HOUSE - RICKY'S BEDROOM - MOMENTS LATER

**On VIDEO:** We're in an empty parking lot on a cold, gray day. Something is floating across from us... it's an empty, wrinkled, white PLASTIC BAG. We follow it as the wind carries it in a circle around us, sometimes whipping it about violently, or, without warning, sending it soaring skyward, then letting it float gracefully down to the ground...

Jane and Ricky sit on the bed, watching his WIDE-SCREEN TV.

>                    RICKY
>           It was one of those days when it's a
>           minute away from snowing. And there's
>           this electricity in the air, you can
>           almost hear it, right? And this bag was
>           just... dancing with me. Like a little
>           kid begging me to play with it. For
>           fifteen minutes. That's the day I
>           realized that there was this entire life
>           behind things, and this incredibly
>           benevolent force that wanted me to know
>           there was no reason to be afraid. Ever.

A beat.

>                    RICKY
>           Video's a poor excuse, I know. But it
>           helps me remember... I need to
>           remember...

Now Jane is watching him.

>                    RICKY
>                 (distant)
>           Sometimes there's so much beauty in the
>           world I feel like I can't take it... and
>           my heart is going to cave in.

After a moment, Jane takes his hand. Then she leans in and kisses him softly on the lips. His eyes scan hers, curious to see how <u>she</u> reacts to this...

>                    JANE
>                 (suddenly)
>           Oh my God. What time is it?

INT. BURNHAM HOUSE - DINING ROOM - MOMENTS LATER

Lester sits at the table in sloppy clothes, eating his dinner voraciously and drinking beer from a bottle. Across from him, Carolyn picks at her food, watching him with contempt. EASY-LISTENING MUSIC plays on the STEREO.

(CONTINUED)

CONTINUED:

We HEAR the back door SLAM, then Jane enters and quickly takes her seat at the table.

                JANE
      Sorry I'm late.

                CAROLYN
        (overly cheerful)
      No, no, that's quite all right, dear.
      Your father and I were just discussing
      his day at work.
        (to Lester)
      Why don't you tell our daughter about it,
      honey?

Jane stares at both her parents, apprehensive. Lester looks at Carolyn darkly, then flashes a "you-asked-for-it" grin.

                LESTER
      Janie, today I quit my job. And then I
      told my boss to fuck himself, and then I
      blackmailed him for almost sixty thousand
      dollars. Pass the asparagus.

                CAROLYN
      Your father seems to think this kind of
      behavior is something to be proud of.

                LESTER
      And your mother seems to prefer I go
      through life like a fucking prisoner
      while she keeps my dick in a mason jar
      under the sink.

                CAROLYN
        (ashen)
      How dare you speak to me that way in
      front of her? And I marvel that you can
      be so contemptuous of me, on the same day
      that you lose your job!

                LESTER
      Lose it? I didn't lose it. It's not like,
      "Oops, where'd my job go?" I quit.
      Someone pass me the asparagus.

                CAROLYN
      Oh! Oh! And I want to thank you for
      putting me under the added pressure of
      being the sole breadwinner now--

                LESTER
      I already have a job.

                     (CONTINUED)

                          CAROLYN
                    (not stopping)
               No, no, don't give a second thought as to
               who's going to pay the mortgage. We'll
               just leave it all up to Carolyn. You
               mean, you're going to take care of
               everything now, Carolyn? Yes. I don't
               mind. I really don't. You mean,
               everything? You don't mind having the
               sole responsibility, your husband feels
               he can just quit his job--

                          LESTER
                    (overlapping)
               Will someone pass me the fucking
               asparagus?

                          JANE
                    (rises)
               Okay, I'm not going to be a part of this--

                          LESTER
                    (means it)
               Sit down.

Jane does so, surprised and intimidated by the power in his
voice. Lester gets up, crosses to the other side of the table
to get a PLATE OF ASPARAGUS, then sits again as he serves
himself.

                          LESTER
               I'm sick and tired of being treated like
               I don't exist. You two do whatever you
               want to do whenever you want to do it and
               I don't complain. All I want is the same
               courtesy--

                          CAROLYN
                    (overlapping)
               Oh, you don't complain? Oh, excuse me.
               Excuse me. I must be psychotic then, if
               you don't complain. What is this?! Am I
               locked away in a padded cell somewhere,
               hallucinating? That's the only
               explanation I can think of--

Lester hurls the plate of asparagus against the wall with
such force it SHATTERS, frightening Carolyn and Jane.

                          LESTER
                    (casual)
               Don't interrupt me, honey.

CONTINUED: (3)

He goes back to eating his meal, as if nothing unusual has happened. Carolyn sits in her chair, shivering with rage. Jane just stares at the plate in front of her.

> LESTER
> Oh, and another thing. From now on, we're going to alternate our dinner music. Because frankly, and I don't think I'm alone here, I'm really tired of this Lawrence Welk shit.

INT. BURNHAM HOUSE - JANE'S BEDROOM - THAT NIGHT

Jane is sitting on her bed. There is a KNOCK at the door.

> JANE
> Go. Away.

> CAROLYN (O.C.)
> Honey, please let me in.

Jane rolls her eyes, crosses to the door and lets Carolyn in.

> CAROLYN
> I wish that you hadn't witnessed that awful scene tonight. But in a way, I'm glad.

> JANE
> Why, so I could see what freaks you and Dad really are?

> CAROLYN
> Me?

She stares at Jane, then starts to cry.

> JANE
> Aw, Christ, Mom.

> CAROLYN
> (tearful)
> No, I'm glad because you're old enough now to learn the most important lesson in life: you cannot count on anyone except yourself.
> (sighs)
> You cannot count on anyone except yourself. It's sad, but true, and the sooner you learn it, the better.

(CONTINUED)

CONTINUED:

                         JANE
               Look, Mom, I really don't feel like
               having a Kodak moment here, okay?

Carolyn suddenly SLAPS Jane, hard.

                         CAROLYN
               You ungrateful little brat. Just look at
               everything you have. When I was your age,
               I lived in a duplex. We didn't even have
               our own house.

Embarrassed, she quickly leaves. Jane looks in a mirror and
rubs her cheek, then crosses to the window and looks out.

EXT. FITTS HOUSE - CONTINUOUS

Jane's POV: We're across from Ricky's room, looking in. He
stands at the window with his DIGICAM, videotaping us. On the
WIDE-SCREEN TV behind him, we see Jane standing in her window
as she looks across at him. She waves. Ricky just keeps
videotaping. A beat, then she starts to take off her shirt.

INT. FITTS HOUSE - RICKY'S BEDROOM - CONTINUOUS

We're behind Ricky as he videotapes Jane in her window. She
has now removed her shirt. She stands there in her bra, then
reaches behind her back to unhook the bra.

On VIDEO: We ZOOM toward her as she takes off her bra
clumsily. She's obviously embarrassed, but she's gone this
far and there's no turning back. She stands there with her
breasts exposed, trying to look defiant, but she's achingly
vulnerable...

Suddenly, the door is thrown open and the Colonel enters,
incensed. Startled, Ricky turns around. As soon as his eyes
meet his father's, he knows what's up.

                         COLONEL
               You little bastard--

Ricky scrambles to dodge his father, but the Colonel is too
fast; he punches Ricky in the face, knocking him to the
floor.

                         COLONEL
               How did you get in there?

EXT. BURNHAM HOUSE - CONTINUOUS

From her window, Jane watches, pulling the drapes in front of
her.

EXT. FITTS HOUSE - CONTINUOUS

Jane's POV: In the WINDOW across from us, the Colonel
proceeds to give Ricky a serious beating, punching his face.

INT. FITTS HOUSE - RICKY'S BEDROOM - CONTINUOUS

Ricky's lip is bleeding, but he maintains a steady gaze at
his father during this violence.

                    COLONEL
               (unnerved)
          How!? How?! C'mon, get up! Fight back,
          you little pussy!

                    RICKY
          No, sir. I won't fight you.

The Colonel grabs him by the collar.

                    COLONEL
          How did you get in there?

                    RICKY
          I picked the lock, sir.

                    COLONEL
          What were you looking for? Money? Are you
          on dope again?

                    RICKY
          No, sir. I wanted to show my girlfriend
          your Nazi plate.

A beat.

                    COLONEL
          Girlfriend?

                    RICKY
          Yes, sir. She lives next door.

The Colonel glances toward the window.

His POV: In the WINDOW across from us, Jane peeks out from
behind the drape. She quickly pulls it shut.

                    RICKY
          Her name's Jane.

A beat. The Colonel is suddenly, deeply shamed.

                                        (CONTINUED)

CONTINUED:

                    COLONEL
          This is for your own good, boy. You have
          no respect for other people's things, for
          authority, for...

                    RICKY
          Sir, I'm sorry.

                    COLONEL
          You can't just go around doing whatever
          you feel like, you can't--there are rules
          in life--

                    RICKY
          Yes, sir.

                    COLONEL
          You need structure, you need discipline--

                    RICKY
               (simultaneous)
          Discipline. Yes, sir, thank you for
          trying to teach me. Don't give up on me,
          Dad.

The Colonel stands, still breathing heavily. Tenderness fills
his face, and he reaches out to touch Ricky's cheek.

                    COLONEL
          Oh, Ricky...

But something keeps him from doing it.

                    COLONEL
          You stay out of there.

He leaves. Ricky gets up and goes to his bureau. He looks at
his reflection in the mirror, calmly takes a cloth and starts
to wipe the blood from his face.

FADE TO BLACK.

In darkness, we HEAR repetitive GUNSHOTS.

FADE IN:

INT. INDOOR FIRING RANGE - ONE MONTH LATER

Carolyn, wearing PROTECTIVE HEADGEAR, is holding a GLOCK 19
AUTOMATIC REVOLVER with both hands, FIRING it directly at us.

She empties a round and stands there, exhilarated. An
ATTENDANT approaches with a new round of ammunition.

                                             (CONTINUED)

CONTINUED:

                        ATTENDANT
                  (loading gun)
            I gotta say, Mrs. Burnham, when you first
            came here I thought you would be
            hopeless. But you're a natural.

                        CAROLYN
            Well, all I know is... I love shooting
            this gun!

And she starts FIRING again.

INT. MERCEDES-BENZ ML320 - LATER

Bobby Darin sings "DON'T RAIN ON MY PARADE" on the RADIO.
Carolyn SINGS along as she drives. Her face has lost its
usual resolute determination; she's actually enjoying herself
spontaneously, and the lack of her usual self-consciousness
allows us to see just how beautiful she is.

ANGLE ON the GLOCK 19 sitting on the passenger seat amidst
some CDs.

Carolyn takes the gun and holds it at arm's length, admiring
it as she continues to SING.

EXT. ROBIN HOOD TRAIL - CONTINUOUS

The Mercedes turns onto Robin Hood Trail.

INT. MERCEDES-BENZ ML320 - CONTINUOUS

Carolyn's POV: We turn into the Burnham driveway. A 1970
PONTIAC FIREBIRD with racing stripes blocks our access to the
garage.

CLOSE on Carolyn: She doesn't like having things in her way.

INT. BURNHAM HOUSE - FAMILY ROOM - MOMENTS LATER

Lester's REMOTE-CONTROLLED MODEL JEEP is zooming across the
floor of the family room, expertly maneuvering corners and
narrowly avoiding crashing.

Lester is sprawled on the couch in his underwear, drinking a
BEER and controlling the car. His working out is beginning to
produce results. The room, too, seems changed: sloppier, more
lived in.

Carolyn enters through the kitchen, flushed and angry. She
just stands there, staring at Lester. After a moment, he
looks up at her.

                                                (CONTINUED)

CONTINUED:

                    LESTER
          What?

                    CAROLYN
          Ah, whose car is that out front?

                    LESTER
          Mine. 1970 Pontiac Firebird. The car I
          always wanted and now I have it. I rule!

                    CAROLYN
          Where's the Camry?

                    LESTER
          I traded it in.

                    CAROLYN
          Shouldn't you have consulted me first?

                    LESTER
          Hmm, let me think... No. You never drove
          it.
               (then)
          Have you done something different? You
          look great.

                    CAROLYN
               (brusque)
          Where's Jane?

                    LESTER
          Jane not home. We have the whole house to
          ourselves.

He smiles at her playfully. She stares back, annoyed. It's
the same look she had at the beginning, when he dropped his
briefcase, but whatever power that look had is gone. Lester
just LAUGHS.

                    LESTER
          Christ, Carolyn. When did you become
          so... joyless?

                    CAROLYN
               (taken aback)
          Joyless?! I am not joyless! There happens
          to be a lot about me that you don't know,
          mister smarty man. There is plenty of joy
          in my life.

                                        (CONTINUED)

CONTINUED: (2)

                    LESTER
              (leaning toward her)
     Whatever happened to that girl who used
     to fake seizures at frat parties when she
     got bored? And who used to run up to the
     roof of our first apartment building to
     flash the traffic helicopters? Have you
     totally forgotten about her? Because I
     haven't.

His face is close to hers, and suddenly the atmosphere is
charged. She pulls back automatically, but it's clear she's
drawn to him. He smiles, and moves even closer, holding his
beer loosely balanced. Then, just before their lips meet...

                    CAROLYN
              (barely audible)
     Lester. You're going to spill beer on the
     couch.

She's immediately sorry she said it, but it's too late. His
smile fades, and the moment is gone.

                    LESTER
     So what? It's just a couch.

                    CAROLYN
     This is a four thousand dollar sofa
     upholstered in Italian silk. This is not
     "just a couch."

                    LESTER
     It's just a couch!

He stands and gestures toward all the things in the room.

                 LESTER (cont'd)
     This isn't <u>life</u>. This is just <u>stuff</u>. And
     it's become more important to you than
     living. Well, honey, that's just nuts.

Carolyn stares at him, on the verge of tears, then turns and
walks out of the room before he can see her cry.

                 LESTER (cont'd)
              (calls after her)
     I'm only trying to help you.

<u>INT. FITTS HOUSE - RICKY'S BEDROOM - NIGHT</u>

**On VIDEO:** Jane lays in Ricky's bed, wearing a tank top. She
glances at us.

                                     (CONTINUED)

CONTINUED:

                JANE
          (shy)
      Don't.

We're watching the WIDE-SCREEN TV in Ricky's room.

A CORD leads from the TV to Ricky's DIGICAM. Ricky holds the
camera, sitting naked in a chair. It's been almost a month
since his father beat him up, and there are still slight
SCARS on his face. He's aiming his camera at Jane.

                RICKY
      Why?

                JANE
          (re: image on TV)
      It's weird, watching myself. I don't like
      how I look.

                RICKY
      I can't believe you don't know how
      beautiful you are.

                JANE
      I'm not going to sit here for that shit.

She gets out of bed, takes his Digicam and focuses it on him.
We see his image on the TV as she videotapes.

                JANE
      Ha. How does it feel now?

                RICKY
      Fine.

                JANE
      You don't feel naked?

                RICKY
      I am naked.

                JANE
      You know what I mean.

Jane ZOOMS in on his face, which remains placid.

                JANE
      Tell me about being in the hospital.

Ricky smiles.

CONTINUED: (2)

                      RICKY
When I was fifteen, my dad caught me
smoking dope. He totally freaked and
decided to send me to military school. I
told you his whole thing about structure
and discipline, right?
        (laughs)
Well, of course, I got kicked out. Dad
and I had this huge fight, and he hit
me... and then the next day at school,
some kid made a crack about my haircut,
and... I just snapped. I wanted to kill
him. And I would have. Killed him. If
they hadn't pulled me off.
        (then)
That's when my dad put me in the
hospital. Then they drugged me up and
left me in there for two years.

                      JANE
Wow. You must really hate him.

                      RICKY
He's not a bad man.

He grabs a half-smoked JOINT from an ashtray and lights it.

                      JANE
Well... you better believe I'd hate my
father if he did something like that to
me.
        (laughs)
Wait. I do hate my father.

                      RICKY
Why?

He passes her the joint, then takes the Digicam and focuses
it on her. We see her image on the TV as he videotapes.

                      JANE
He's a total asshole and he's got this
crush on my friend Angela and it's
disgusting.

                      RICKY
You'd rather he had the crush on you?

                      JANE
Gross, no! But it'd be nice if I was
anywhere near as important to him as she
is.
        (then)
        (MORE)

CONTINUED: (3)

>                    JANE (cont'd)
>           I know you think my dad's harmless, but
>           you're wrong. He's doing massive
>           psychological damage to me.

>                    RICKY
>           How?

Jane looks into the camera, a loopy, stoned grin on her face.

>                    JANE (cont'd)
>           Well, now, I too need structure. A little
>           fucking discipline.

They LAUGH. She lays back on the bed.

>                    JANE
>           I'm serious, though. How could he not be
>           damaging me? I need a father who's a role
>           model, not some horny geek-boy who's
>           gonna spray his shorts whenever I bring a
>           girlfriend home from school.
>                (snorts)
>           What a lame-o. Somebody really should put
>           him out of his misery.

Her mind wanders for a beat.

>                    RICKY
>           Want me to kill him for you?

Jane looks at him and sits up.

>                    JANE
>           Yeah, would you?

>                    RICKY
>                (smiles)
>           It'll cost you.

>                    JANE
>           Well, I've been baby-sitting since I was
>           about ten. I've got almost three thousand
>           dollars. 'Course, I was saving it up for
>           a boob job.

She stands and sticks out her breasts, then falls back on the
bed, LAUGHING.

>                    JANE
>           But my tits can wait, huh?

>                    RICKY
>           You know, that's not a very nice thing to
>           do, hiring somebody to kill your dad.

CONTINUED: (4)

> JANE
> Well, I guess I'm just not a very nice
> girl, then, am I?

She smiles dreamily at him. He turns the Digicam off and the
TV screen goes BLUE. He lowers the camera and looks at her
intently.

> JANE
> (suddenly nervous)
> You know I'm not serious, right?

> RICKY
> Of course.

He puts the Digicam down and joins Jane on the bed. A long
moment where neither of them speaks. He caresses her hair,
gazing into her eyes.

> RICKY
> Do you know how lucky we are to have
> found each other?

FADE TO BLACK.

FADE IN:

EXT. ROBIN HOOD TRAIL - EARLY MORNING

We're FLYING above Robin Hood Trail. We see the BURNHAM'S
HOUSE below us as we APPROACH it steadily.

> LESTER
> Remember those posters that said, "Today
> is the first day of the rest of your
> life?" Well, that's true of every day
> except one.
> (a beat)
> The day you die.

We're almost on top of the Burnham house now, as Lester,
wearing sweatpants and running shoes, bursts out of the front
door and dashes up the driveway.

EXT. ROBIN HOOD TRAIL - A SHORT TIME LATER

We're now at street level, as Lester runs toward us. He
carries a WALKMAN and wears EARPHONES, and we HEAR ROCK MUSIC
as he runs. The endorphins have kicked in, and Lester grins,
reveling in the sheer physical pleasure of his body.

<u>INT. BURNHAM HOUSE - KITCHEN - A SHORT TIME LATER</u>

The blender GRINDS as Lester, still in his sweatpants, makes himself a high-protein shake. He's in excellent shape; even his posture has changed, and he moves with the confident, easy swagger of an athlete. Jane watches him blankly from the kitchen table.

Carolyn enters. Lester leans against the counter, drinking his shake directly from the blender pitcher, eyeing her. He's got a newfound sexual energy that makes her uncomfortable, and he knows it. Carolyn quickly rinses off her coffee cup, avoiding his eyes, and starts out.

> CAROLYN
> Jane, hurry up. I've got a very important appointment--

> JANE
> Mom, is it okay if Angela sleeps over tonight?

Jane looks at Lester to see how he reacts. He doesn't.

> CAROLYN
> Well, of course, she's always welcome.
> (on her way out)
> You know, I thought maybe you two had a fight. I haven't seen her around here in a while.

And she's gone. Jane continues staring at her father. Finally, he glances over at her.

> LESTER
> What?

> JANE
> (nervous)
> I've been too embarrassed to bring her over. Because of you, and the way that you behave.

> LESTER
> What are you talking about? I've barely even spoken to her.

> JANE
> (angry)
> Dad! You stare at her all the time, like you're drunk! It's disgusting!

(CONTINUED)

CONTINUED:

          LESTER
      (angry himself)
  You better watch yourself, Janie, or
  you're going to turn into a real bitch,
  just like your mother.

Jane is stunned. She quickly rises, trying to get out of the
kitchen before she starts crying.

ANGLE on Lester, and the immediate regret in his eyes.

          LESTER
      (under his breath)
  Fuck.

INT. FITTS HOUSE - UPSTAIRS HALLWAY - CONTINUOUS

We're outside Ricky's room, MOVING slowly toward the open
door, through which we can see Ricky, standing at his bureau
mirror, combing his hair. The scars on his face are almost
gone now.

A REVERSE ANGLE reveals the Colonel standing outside the door
looking in, watching Ricky with great tenderness. Then Ricky
looks up at him, and the Colonel is suddenly self-conscious.

          COLONEL
      (brusque)
  You ready to go?

          RICKY
  Oh, I don't need a ride. I'm going to go
  in with Jane and her mom.

EXT. FITTS HOUSE - FRONT PORCH - MOMENTS LATER

Ricky emerges from the house, followed by the Colonel, who
watches his son as he heads toward the Burnham house.

His POV: Carolyn waves from the Mercedes, flashing an
insincere smile. Jane leans forward from the passenger seat
and glares at us. As Ricky starts to get in the car, Lester
emerges from the house in his sweatpants.

          LESTER
  Yo, Ricky. How's it going?

          RICKY
  Pretty decent, Mr. Burnham.

Ricky pulls his door shut, but not before Lester mouths "call
me" and Ricky gives a slight nod in acknowledgment.

(CONTINUED)

CONTINUED:


CLOSE on the Colonel's face: he looks confused.

As the Mercedes backs out of the driveway, Lester glances over at him.

Lester's POV: The Colonel watches the car driving off, then looks at us. His face tightens.

Lester studies him for a moment, then grins and salutes before going inside the house.

CLOSE on the Colonel, deeply troubled.

INT. FITTS HOUSE - RICKY'S ROOM - MOMENTS LATER

The door swings open silently and the Colonel enters. He starts going through Ricky's bureau. He opens the DRAWER in which we know Ricky keeps his marijuana, but he doesn't discover its false bottom. He stands and looks around, his eyes finally landing on:

The DIGICAM and a stack of CASSETTES on a shelf. The camera is still connected to the TV.

The Colonel turns on the TV, examines the Digicam and presses "play." The TV's blank screen suddenly gives way to...

On VIDEO: Barbara Fitts sits at the kitchen table, staring off into space.

The Colonel watches, at first baffled, then impatient. He takes the cassette out of the Digicam and inserts another. On the TV screen we see...

On VIDEO: Through the Burnham's GARAGE WINDOW, we see Lester step out of his pants and briefs. Then, naked except for his black socks, he grabs the dumbbells and starts lifting them, watching his reflection in the window as he does...

The Colonel sinks slowly onto Ricky's bed, mesmerized.

INT. MR. SMILEY'S - LATER

Lester, wearing a Mr. Smiley's uniform, is happily flipping burgers on a grill.

> CO-WORKER
> Hey Lester, I need that Super Smiley with cheese, A.S.A.P.

> LESTER
> You need more than that, my little hombre.

CONTINUED:


Lester looks up suddenly when he HEARS:

                    CAROLYN (O.C.)
               (over speakers)
          What's good here?

                    BUDDY (O.C.)
               (over speakers)
          Nothing.

                    CAROLYN (O.C.)
               (over speakers)
          Then I guess we'll just have to be bad,
          won't we?
               (then)
          I think I'll have a double Smiley
          Sandwich and curly fries, and a vanilla
          shake.

                    BUDDY (O.C.)
               (over speakers)
          Make that two.

                    COUNTER GIRL (O.C.)
               (over speakers)
          Please drive around thank you.

Lester's face darkens, then... he smiles. He puts his spatula
down.

EXT. MR. SMILEY'S - CONTINUOUS

The Mercedes pulls around to the DRIVE-THRU WINDOW. Carolyn
drives; Buddy sits beside her.

                    CAROLYN
          I think we deserve a little junk food,
          after the workout we had this morning.

                    BUDDY
               (nuzzles her neck)
          I'm flattered.

They are too involved with each other to notice Lester
watching them from the drive-thru window.

                    LESTER
               (overly cheerful)
          Smile! You're at Mr. Smiley's!

Carolyn almost jumps out of her skin.

                                        (CONTINUED)

CONTINUED:

Lester leans out of the drive-thru window, grinning at her,
holding bags filled with fast food. The Counter Girl stands
next to him, staring blankly.

                  LESTER
    Would you like to try our new beef and
    cheese pot pie on a stick, just a dollar
    ninety-nine for a limited time only?

Carolyn struggles to appear nonchalant.

                  CAROLYN
      (re: Buddy)
    We were just at a seminar.
      (then, all business)
    Buddy, this is my--

                  LESTER
    Her _husband_. We've met before, but
    something tells me you're going to
    remember me this time.

                  COUNTER GIRL
      (to Carolyn)
    Whoa. You are so busted.

                  CAROLYN
      (flustered)
    You know, this really doesn't concern
    you.

                  LESTER
    Actually, Janeane is senior drive-thru
    manager, so you kind of are on her turf.
      (to Carolyn, quietly)
    So. This makes sense.

                  CAROLYN
      (miserable)
    Oh, Lester--

                  LESTER
    Honey, it's okay. I want you to be happy.
      (then)
    Would you like Smiley Sauce with that?

                  CAROLYN
    Lester, just stop it!

                  LESTER
    Uh-uh. You don't get to tell me what to
    do. Ever again.

CONTINUED: (2)

Carolyn closes her eyes, defeated, then grabs the wheel,
shifts gears and drives off.

EXT. TOP HAT MOTEL - A SHORT TIME LATER

The sky is filled with ominous gray clouds. Wind whips
garbage across the parking lot as Carolyn's Mercedes pulls in
next to Buddy's Jaguar.

INT. MERCEDES-BENZ ML320 - CONTINUOUS

Carolyn grips the wheel tightly, staring straight ahead.
Buddy looks at her unhappily.

> BUDDY
> I'm sorry. I guess we should cool it for
> a while. I'm facing a potentially very
> expensive divorce.

> CAROLYN
> Oh, no. I understand completely.
> (sarcastic)
> In order to be successful, one must
> project an image of success. At all
> times.

She regrets it the second it's out of her mouth, and turns to
him. He just looks at her sadly, then gets out of the car and
shuts the door. She starts to CRY. As before, she SLAPS
herself, hard.

> CAROLYN
> Stop it. Stop it!

She closes her eyes tight, trying to stop the tears, then
suddenly SCREAMS as loud as she can.

EXT. TOP HAT MOTEL - CONTINUOUS

Buddy's Jaguar speeds off, leaving the Mercedes alone in the
parking lot. We can still HEAR Carolyn's muffled SCREAMING.
There is a sound of distant THUNDER.

INT. BURNHAM HOUSE - GARAGE - THAT NIGHT

It's RAINING outside. We HEAR ROCK MUSIC as Lester pumps
iron. He puts the weights down and looks at his REFLECTION in
the window:

His POV: His arms are pumped. He smiles.

CONTINUED:

He reaches under the bench and grabs a CIGAR BOX. Opening it, he digs through MARIJUANA PARAPHERNALIA, only to pull out an empty ZIP-LOC BAG.

                    LESTER
          Shit.

INT. FITTS HOUSE - KITCHEN - MOMENTS LATER

Ricky and the Colonel sit at the table, eating in silence. Barbara rinses off a pan at the sink, then stares at it as if she can't quite remember what she meant to do with it. We suddenly HEAR a BEEPING noise. Ricky pulls his BEEPER off his belt and checks it.

                    RICKY
               (getting up)
          I have to run next door. Jane left her
          geometry book in my bag and she needs it
          to do her homework.

He heads into the hall. The Colonel watches him go, uneasy.

INT. ANGELA'S BMW - CONTINUOUS

Angela drives, squinting through the windshield as the wipers move back and forth.

                    ANGELA
          So you and psycho boy are fucking on
          like, a regular basis now, right?

                    JANE
               (irritable)
          No.

                    ANGELA
          Oh, come on. You can tell me. Does he
          have a big dick?

                    JANE
          Look, I'm not gonna talk about his dick
          with you, okay? It's not like that.

                    ANGELA
          Not like what? Doesn't he have one?
               (then)
          Why don't you want to talk about it? I
          mean, I tell you every single detail
          about every guy that I fuck.

                                        (CONTINUED)

CONTINUED:

>          JANE
> Yeah, and maybe you shouldn't, all right?
> Maybe I don't really want to hear all
> that.

>          ANGELA
> Oh, so now that you have a boyfriend,
> you're like, above it?
>          (rolls her eyes)
> We gotta get you a real man.

INT. FITTS HOUSE - KITCHEN - CONTINUOUS

The Colonel rinses off his plate at the sink. Something
outside catches his eye, and he cranes his neck to get a
better look at...

His POV: Through the window over the sink, we can see into
the Burnham's GARAGE WINDOW. Our view is blurred by the RAIN,
but we see Lester, his upper body pumped and glistening in
sweat as he counts out a wad of BILLS... and then Ricky walks
into view.

The Colonel's face tightens.

His POV: Lester drapes his arm around Ricky as he gives him
the money. We can only see Lester from the waist up, so he
looks naked.

INT. BURNHAM HOUSE - GARAGE - CONTINUOUS

Ricky, his hair wet from the rain, puts the cash in his
pocket. Lester's arm remains draped around his shoulder.

>          RICKY
>          (grins)
> You got any papers?

>          LESTER
> Yeah, in the cigar box, right over there.
>          (laughs)
> You know, put up a fight, dude! You are
> such a pushover. "No I can't. Really.
> Okay."

And he slaps Ricky playfully on the chest. Ricky grins, then
squats down and reaches under the weight bench.

>          RICKY
> You should learn to roll a joint.

Lester sits in the bowl chair and leans back, his hands
behind his head, watching Ricky roll the joint.

<u>INT. FITTS HOUSE - KITCHEN - CONTINUOUS</u>

The Colonel's POV: Lester leans back in his chair. We see
only Ricky's back and shoulders as he rolls the joint. After
a beat, Lester's jaw drops, then he throws his head back.
From our perspective, it looks very much like Ricky is giving
Lester a blow job.

The Colonel watches, incredulous. Then we HEAR a CAR
APPROACHING, and the Colonel glances over at:

His POV: Angela's BMW pulls into the driveway, stopping
behind Lester's Firebird. As Angela and Jane get out and run
toward the house, our focus MOVES back to the GARAGE WINDOW.
Ricky stands, looking a little panicked. Lester pulls on his
T-shirt, and both he and Ricky cross out of view.

<u>INT. BURNHAM HOUSE - KITCHEN - MOMENTS LATER</u>

Lester leans nonchalantly against the counter. Jane and
Angela enter. Jane frowns when she sees him.

                    LESTER
          Oh. Hi.

                    JANE
          Where's Mom?

                    LESTER
          Don't know.

                    ANGELA
          Hi, Mr. Burnham.

                    LESTER
          Hi.

He's trying to remain cool, and doing a pretty good job.

                    ANGELA
          Wow. Look at you. Have you been working
          out?

                    LESTER
          Some.

Jane rolls her eyes and exits. Angela walks over to Lester.

                    ANGELA
          You can really tell. Look at those arms.

She places her hand on his arm flirtatiously, looks up at him
and smiles, fully expecting to intimidate him by doing so.

(CONTINUED)

CONTINUED:

But something has changed, and he isn't intimidated at all.
He looks directly back at her, leans in and smiles slowly.

                    LESTER
          You like muscles?

His voice is low and intense. She moves away, suddenly
insecure.

                    ANGELA
          I--I should probably go see what Jane's
          up to.

And she heads out quickly. Lester watches her go, baffled.

INT. FITTS HOUSE - RICKY'S ROOM - CONTINUOUS

Ricky enters, wet from the pouring rain, and crosses to his
bureau, pulling the wad of CASH out of his pocket as he goes.

                    COLONEL (O.C.)
          Where'd you get that?

Ricky turns, startled.

His POV: The Colonel steps out of the shadows.

Ricky takes a step back.

                    RICKY
          From my job.

                    COLONEL
          Don't lie to me.
             (beat)
          I saw you with him.

                    RICKY
             (incredulous)
          You were watching me?

                    COLONEL
          What did he make you do?

                    RICKY
             (laughs)
          Dad, you don't really think... me and Mr.
          Burnham?

                    COLONEL
             (furious)
          Don't you laugh at me!
             (then)
                    (MORE)

(CONTINUED)

CONTINUED:

                    COLONEL (cont'd)
          I will not sit back and watch my only son
          become a cocksucker!

                    RICKY
          Jesus, what is with you--

The Colonel BACKHANDS Ricky so hard it sends the boy
sprawling.

                    COLONEL
          I swear to God, I will throw you out of
          this house and never look at you again.

                    RICKY
               (taken aback)
          You mean that?

                    COLONEL
          Damn straight I do. I'd rather you were
          dead than be a fucking faggot.

A beat. Ricky suddenly smiles. He gets up.

                    RICKY
          You're right. I suck dick for money.

                    COLONEL
          Boy--

                    RICKY
          Two thousand dollars. I'm that good.

                    COLONEL
          Get out.

                    RICKY
          And you should see me fuck. I'm the best
          piece of ass in three states.

                    COLONEL
               (explodes)
          Get out!! I don't ever want to see you
          again!!

Ricky eyes the Colonel. He's finally discovered a way to
break free from his father, and he can't believe it was this
simple.

                    RICKY
          What a sad old man you are.

                    COLONEL
               (a whisper)
          Get out.

                                        (CONTINUED)

CONTINUED: (2)

Ricky grabs his backpack, turns and walks out the door, leaving the Colonel standing there, glassy-eyed and breathing heavily.

INT. FITTS HOUSE - KITCHEN - MOMENTS LATER

Ricky enters to discover Barbara standing in the middle of the room, clutching a dish, frightened. She's obviously heard his argument with his father, and she looks into his eyes, searching, aware that something eventful is taking place.

                    RICKY
          Mom, I'm leaving.

A beat.

                    BARBARA
          Okay, wear a raincoat.

                    RICKY
              (hugs her)
          I wish things would have been better for
          you. Take care of Dad.

He kisses her cheek softly, then exits out the back door, leaving her standing alone, still clutching her dish.

INT. FITTS HOUSE - RICKY'S BEDROOM - CONTINUOUS

The Colonel's POV: Below us, Ricky dashes through the rain to the Burnham's front door and knocks. Lester opens it and lets him in.

EXT. FITTS HOUSE - CONTINUOUS

The Colonel looks coldly down at us from Ricky's bedroom window, and then he pulls the drapes shut.

EXT. FREEWAY - CONTINUOUS

The MERCEDES-BENZ ML320 is parked in the breakdown lane, its HAZARD LIGHTS BLINKING. Cars ZOOM past in the rain.

INT. MERCEDES-BENZ ML320 - CONTINUOUS

Carolyn sits behind the wheel, listening to a MOTIVATIONAL TAPE on the STEREO.

                    TAPE VOICE
          --disinvesting problems of their power,
          and removing their ability to make us
          afraid. This is the secret to "me-
          centered" living.
              (MORE)

                                        (CONTINUED)

CONTINUED:

> TAPE VOICE (cont'd)
> Only by taking full responsibility for
> your problems--<u>and</u> their solutions--will
> you ever be able to break free from the
> constant cycle of victimhood.

Carolyn leans over and opens the glove compartment. She takes
out her GLOCK 19.

> TAPE VOICE (cont'd)
> Remember, you are only a victim if you
> <u>choose</u> to be a victim...

INT. BURNHAM HOUSE - JANE'S ROOM - CONTINUOUS

Angela is sprawled across the bed. Jane stands across the
room from her.

> JANE
> I don't think we could be friends
> anymore.

> ANGELA
> You are way too uptight about sex.

> JANE
> Just don't fuck my dad, all right?
> Please?

> ANGELA
> Why not?

There is a KNOCK on the door. Jane sits up, alarmed.

> JANE
> (angry)
> Dad! Leave us alone!

> RICKY (O.C.)
> It's me.

Jane jumps up and opens the door and lets him in.

> RICKY (cont'd)
> (to Jane)
> If I had to leave tonight, would you come
> with me?

> JANE
> What?

> RICKY
> If I had to go to New York. To live.
> Tonight. Would you come with me?

CONTINUED:

                JANE
Yes.


               ANGELA
You guys can't be serious.
    (to Jane)
You're just a kid. And he's like, a
mental case. You'll end up living in a
box on the street.


                JANE
I'm no more a kid than you are!
    (to Ricky)
We can use my plastic surgery money.


               RICKY
We won't have to. I have over forty
thousand dollars. And I know people in
the city who can help us get set up.


               ANGELA
What, other drug dealers?


               RICKY
Yes.


               ANGELA
Jane, you'd be out of your mind to go
with him.


                JANE
Why do you even care?


               ANGELA
Because you're my friend!


               RICKY
She's not your friend. She's somebody you
use to feel better about yourself.


               ANGELA
Go fuck yourself, psycho!


                JANE
You shut up, bitch!


               ANGELA
Jane! He is a freak!

CONTINUED: (2)

> JANE
> Well, then so am I! And we'll always be
> freaks and we'll never be like other
> people. And you'll never be a freak
> because you're just too perfect.

> ANGELA
> Oh, yeah? Well, at least I'm not ugly.

> RICKY
> Yes, you are. And you're boring. And
> you're totally ordinary. And you know it.

Angela stares at him, stunned, then starts toward the door.

> ANGELA
> You two deserve each other.

And she exits, SLAMMING the door behind her. Jane turns to
Ricky and he takes her in his arms.

INT. BURNHAM HOUSE - UPSTAIRS HALLWAY - CONTINUOUS

Angela sits on the stairs, shaken, crying.

EXT. BURNHAM HOUSE - GARAGE - CONTINUOUS

We're MOVING SLOWLY toward the Burnham's GARAGE WINDOW
through the RAIN. Through the window, we see Lester, wearing
only his sweatpants, performing bench presses.

INT. BURNHAM HOUSE - GARAGE - CONTINUOUS

Through the window, we see the Colonel standing outside,
watching. We ZOOM slowly in on him as he watches, transfixed.

EXT. BURNHAM HOUSE - GARAGE - CONTINUOUS

His POV: Lester finishes his last rep, then racks the weights
and sits up, sweaty and out of breath. He runs his free hand
over his chest... and then he glances at us, suddenly aware
he's being watched.

INT. BURNHAM HOUSE - GARAGE - CONTINUOUS

Lester and the Colonel stare at each other through the
window.

EXT. BURNHAM HOUSE - GARAGE - MOMENTS LATER

The RAIN is coming down in sheets now, and there is a sharp
CLAP of THUNDER. We're directly outside the GARAGE DOOR as it
slowly lifts to reveal Lester smiling at us.

(CONTINUED)

CONTINUED:

                     LESTER
         Jesus, man. You're soaked.

INT. BURNHAM HOUSE - GARAGE - CONTINUOUS

Lester pulls the Colonel inside. The Colonel moves stiffly
and seems preoccupied, slightly disoriented.

                     LESTER
         You want me to get Ricky? He's in Jane's
         room.

The Colonel just stands there, looking at Lester.

                     LESTER
         You okay?

                    COLONEL
          (his voice thick)
         Where's your wife?

                     LESTER
         Uh... I don't know. Probably out fucking
         that dorky prince of real estate asshole.
         And you know what? I don't care.

The Colonel moves closer towards him.

                    COLONEL
         Your wife is with another man and you
         don't care?

                     LESTER
         Nope, our marriage is just for show. A
         commercial, for how normal we are. When
         we are anything but.

He grins... and so does the Colonel.

                     LESTER
         You're shaking.

He places his hand on the Colonel's shoulder. The Colonel
closes his eyes.

                     LESTER
          We really should get you out of these
         clothes.

                    COLONEL
          (a whisper)
         Yes...

CONTINUED:

He opens his eyes and looks at Lester, his face filled with
an anguished vulnerability we wouldn't have thought possible
from him. His eyes are brimming with tears. Lester leans in,
concerned.

                    LESTER
          It's okay.

                    COLONEL
               (hoarse)
          I...

                    LESTER
               (softly)
          Just tell me what you need.

The Colonel reaches up and places his hand on Lester's
cheek... and then kisses him. Lester is momentarily stunned,
and then he pushes the Colonel away. The Colonel's face
crumples in shame.

                    LESTER
          Whoa, whoa, whoa. I'm sorry. You got the
          wrong idea.

The Colonel stares at the floor, blinking, and then he turns
and runs out the open garage door into the rainy night.

INT. MERCEDES-BENZ ML320 - CONTINUOUS

Carolyn is still listening to the same MOTIVATIONAL TAPE. She
holds the GLOCK in her hand.

                    TAPE VOICE
          "I refuse to be a victim." When this
          becomes your mantra, constantly running
          through your head--

Carolyn switches the TAPE OFF and puts the gun in her purse.

                    CAROLYN
          I refuse to be a victim.

EXT. FREEWAY - CONTINUOUS

The Mercedes pulls away from the shoulder.

INT. BURNHAM HOUSE - KITCHEN - CONTINUOUS

Lester enters, opens the refrigerator and grabs a BEER.
Suddenly we HEAR MUSIC coming from the other room. Lester
opens his beer and starts toward the family room.

INT. BURNHAM HOUSE - FAMILY ROOM - CONTINUOUS

His POV: As we MOVE SLOWLY around a corner, Angela comes into view, standing at the STEREO, holding a CD case. She's been crying; her face is puffy, and her hair mussed. She regards us apprehensively... then puts on a slightly defiant smile.

                    ANGELA
          I hope you don't mind if I play the
          stereo.

Lester leans against the wall and takes a swig of his beer.

                    LESTER
          Not at all.
              (then)
          Bad night?

                    ANGELA
          Not really bad, just... strange.

                    LESTER
              (grins)
          Believe me. It couldn't possibly be any
          stranger than mine.

She smiles. They stand there in silence; the atmosphere is charged.

                    ANGELA
          Jane and I had a fight.
              (after a beat)
          It was about you.

She's trying to be seductive as she says this, but she's pretty bad at it. Lester raises his eyebrows.

                    ANGELA
          She's mad at me because I said I think
          you're sexy.

Lester grins. He is sexy.

                    LESTER
              (offering beer)
          Do you want a sip?

She nods. Lester holds the bottle up to her mouth and she drinks clumsily. He gently wipes her chin with the back of his hand.

                                        (CONTINUED)

CONTINUED:

                    LESTER
          So... are you going to tell me? What you
          want?

                    ANGELA
          I don't know.

                    LESTER
          You don't know?

His face is very close to hers. She's unnerved--this is
happening too fast...

                    ANGELA
          What do you want?

                    LESTER
          Are you kidding? I want you. I've wanted
          you since the first moment I saw you. You
          are the most beautiful thing I have ever
          seen.

Angela takes a deep breath just before Lester leans in to
kiss her cheek, her forehead, her eyelids, her neck...

                    ANGELA
          You don't think I'm ordinary?

                    LESTER
          You couldn't be ordinary if you tried.

                    ANGELA
          Thank you.
               (far away)
          I don't think there's anything worse than
          being ordinary...

And Lester kisses her on the lips.

INT. MERCEDES-BENZ ML320 - CONTINUOUS

Carolyn drives, her face resolute.

                    CAROLYN
          I refuse to be a victim. I refuse to be a
          victim. I refuse to be a victim...
               (angry)
          Lester, I have something I have to say to
          you...

INT. BURNHAM HOUSE - FAMILY ROOM - MOMENTS LATER

Angela lays back on the couch as Lester moves in over her. He pulls her jeans off and gently brushes his fingers over her legs, then moves up and caresses her face...

INT. BURNHAM HOUSE - JANE'S ROOM - CONTINUOUS

Ricky and Jane, fully clothed, lie curled up on Jane's bed.

                    JANE
          Are you scared?

                    RICKY
          I don't get scared.

                    JANE
          My parents will try to find me.

                    RICKY
          Mine won't.

INT. BURNHAM HOUSE - FAMILY ROOM - CONTINUOUS

Lester starts unbuttoning Angela's blouse. She seems disconnected from what's happening. Lester pulls her blouse open, exposing her breasts.

Lester looks down at her, grinning, unable to believe he's actually about to do what he's dreamed of so many times, and then...

                    ANGELA
          This is my first time.

Lester LAUGHS.

                    LESTER
          You're kidding.

                    ANGELA
              (a whisper)
          I'm sorry.

A beat. Lester looks down at her, his grin fading.

His POV: Angela lies beneath us, embarrassed and vulnerable. This is not the mythically carnal creature of Lester's fantasies; this is a nervous child.

(CONTINUED)

CONTINUED:

                    ANGELA
          I still want to do it... I just thought I
          should tell you... in case you wondered
          why I wasn't... better.

Lester's face falls. There's no way he's going to go through
with this now.

                    ANGELA
               (confused)
          What's wrong? I thought you said I was
          beautiful.

                    LESTER
               (tenderly)
          You <u>are</u> beautiful.

He grabs a blanket from the back of the couch and drapes it
around her shoulders, covering her nakedness.

                    LESTER
          You are so beautiful... and I would be a
          very lucky man...

He smiles and shakes his head. Humiliated, Angela starts to
cry.

                    ANGELA
          I feel so stupid.

                    LESTER
          Don't.

He hugs her, letting her put her head on his shoulder,
stroking her hair and rocking her gently.

                    ANGELA
          I'm sorry.

Lester takes her by the shoulders and looks at her, serious.

                    LESTER
          You have nothing to be sorry about.

But she keeps crying. Lester hugs her again. We HEAR a loud
CLAP of THUNDER outside.

                    LESTER
               (smiles)
          It's okay. Everything's okay.

EXT. ROBIN HOOD TRAIL - MOMENTS LATER

The Mercedes pulls onto Robin Hood Trail.

INT. MERCEDES-BENZ ML320 - CONTINUOUS

CLOSE on Carolyn's eyes, reflected in the REAR-VIEW MIRROR.
She turns her head to look out the window:

Her POV: The RED DOOR of the Burnham house stands out, even
in the pouring rain.

INT. BURNHAM HOUSE - KITCHEN - MOMENTS LATER

Angela, once again fully clothed, sits at the kitchen
counter. She's eating a turkey sandwich.

                    ANGELA
              Wow. I was starving.

Lester puts a jar of mayonnaise back in the refrigerator.

                    LESTER
              Do you want me to make you another one?

                    ANGELA
              No, no, no. I'm fine.

He turns to her and cocks an eyebrow.

                    LESTER
                  (concerned)
              You sure?

                    ANGELA
              I mean, I'm still a little weirded out,
              but...
                  (sincerely)
              ...I feel better. Thanks.

A long beat, as Lester studies her, then:

                    LESTER
              How's Jane?

                    ANGELA
              What do you mean?

                    LESTER
              I mean, how's her life? Is she happy? Is
              she miserable? I'd really like to know,
              and she'd die before she'd ever tell me
              about it.

                                        (CONTINUED)

CONTINUED:


Angela shifts uncomfortably.

                    ANGELA
          She's... she's really happy. She thinks
          she's in love.

Angela rolls her eyes at how silly this notion is.

                    LESTER
               (quietly)
          Good for her.

An awkward beat.

                    ANGELA
          How are you?

                    LESTER
               (smiles, taken aback)
          God, it's been a long time since anybody
          asked me that.
               (thinks about it)
          I'm great.

They just sit there, smiling at each other, then:

                    ANGELA
               (suddenly)
          I've gotta go to the bathroom.

She crosses off. Lester watches her go, then stands there
wondering why he should suddenly feel so content.

                    LESTER
               (laughs)
          I'm great.

Something at the edge of the counter catches his eye, and he
reaches for...

CLOSE on a framed PHOTOGRAPH as he picks it up: It's the
photo we saw earlier of him, Carolyn and Jane, taken several
years ago at an amusement park. It's startling how happy they
look.

Lester crosses to the kitchen table, where he sits and
studies the photo. He suddenly seems older, more mature...
and then he smiles: the deep, satisfied smile of a man who
just now understands the punch line of a joke he heard long
ago...

CONTINUED: (2)

                         LESTER
              Man oh man...
                   (softly)
              Man oh man oh man...

After a beat, the barrel of a GUN rises up behind his head,
aimed at the base of his skull.

ANGLE ON an arrangement of fresh-cut ROSES in a vase on the
opposite counter, deep crimson against the WHITE TILE WALL.
Then a GUNSHOT suddenly rings out, ECHOING unnaturally.
Instantly, the tile is sprayed with BLOOD, the same deep
crimson as the roses.

INT. BURNHAM HOUSE - FOYER - MOMENTS LATER

Ricky comes down the stairs, followed by Jane.

INT. BURNHAM HOUSE - KITCHEN - MOMENTS LATER

Ricky opens the door from the dining room, then stops. Jane
appears behind him.

                    JANE
              Oh God.

Their POV: A pool of blood is forming on the kitchen table.

Ricky comes into the kitchen and slowly approaches Lester's
lifeless body, wide-eyed but not afraid. Jane follows him, in
shock. Ricky kneels, gazing at Lester's unseen face... then
he smiles, ever so slightly.

His POV: Lester looks back at us; his eyes are lifeless, but
he's smiling the same slight smile.

                         RICKY
                   (an awed whisper)
              Wow.

                         LESTER (V.O.)
              I had always heard your entire life
              flashes in front of your eyes the second
              before you die.

EXT. SKY - DAY

We're FLYING across a white blanket of clouds.

                         LESTER (V.O.)
              First of all, that one second isn't a
              second at all, it stretches on forever,
              like an ocean of time...

EXT. WOODS - NIGHT

In BLACK & WHITE: Eleven-year-old Lester looks up, pointing
excitedly at:

His POV: A DOT OF LIGHT falls across an unbelievably starry
sky.

                    LESTER (V.O.)
          For me, it was lying on my back at Boy
          Scout camp, watching falling stars...

INT. BURNHAM HOUSE - JANE'S BEDROOM - NIGHT

Ricky and Jane lie curled up on Jane's bed, fully clothed. We
HEAR a GUNSHOT from downstairs. They look at each other,
alarmed.

EXT. SUBURBAN STREET - DUSK

In BLACK & WHITE: Maple trees in autumn. Ghostly LEAVES
FLUTTER slowly toward pavement.

                    LESTER (V.O.)
          And yellow leaves, from the maple trees,
          that lined my street...

INT. BURNHAM HOUSE - POWDER ROOM - NIGHT

Angela stands in front of the mirror, fixing her make-up. We
HEAR the GUNSHOT again. Angela turns, frightened.

INT. SUBURBAN HOUSE - DAY

In BLACK & WHITE: CLOSE on an ancient woman's papery HANDS as
they button a cardigan sweater.

                    LESTER (V.O.)
          Or my grandmother's hands, and the way
          her skin seemed like paper...

EXT. BURNHAM HOUSE - NIGHT

Carolyn walks slowly toward the RED DOOR, drenched to the
bone, clutching her PURSE tightly. We HEAR the GUNSHOT again.

EXT. SUBURB - DAY

In BLACK & WHITE: A 1970 PONTIAC FIREBIRD in the driveway of
a suburban home. The SUN'S REFLECTION in the windshield
FLASHES BRILLIANTLY.

(CONTINUED)

CONTINUED:

                         LESTER (V.O.)
                And the first time I saw my cousin Tony's
                brand new Firebird...

INT. FITTS HOUSE - THE COLONEL'S STUDY - NIGHT

The Colonel enters, wet. He's wearing LATEX GLOVES. BLOOD
covers the front of his T-shirt. He paces in front of one of
his GUN CASES; the GLASS DOOR is open, and a gun is
conspicuously missing from inside.

INT. BURNHAM HOUSE - HALL - NIGHT

In BLACK & WHITE: Jane opens her bedroom door, staring at us.

                         LESTER (V.O.)
                And Janie...

EXT. SUBURBAN HOUSE - DUSK

In BLACK & WHITE: A door opens to reveal 4-YEAR-OLD JANE,
dressed for Halloween in a Princess costume, holding a lit
SPARKLER aloft and smiling shyly at us.

                         LESTER (V.O.)
                And Janie...

INT. BURNHAM HOUSE - MASTER BEDROOM - NIGHT

Carolyn enters, terrified, still clutching her PURSE. She
shuts the door and locks it, then takes the GLOCK 19 out of
her purse. She opens the closet door and shoves the gun into
a HAMPER. Then, suddenly aware of Lester's scent, she grabs
as many of his clothes as she can and pulls them to her,
burying her face in them. She sinks to her knees, pulling
several items of clothing down with her, and she begins to
cry.

EXT. AMUSEMENT PARK - NIGHT

In BLACK & WHITE:

A younger Carolyn sits across from us in one of those
SPINNING-TEACUP RIDES, LAUGHING uncontrollably as she twists
the wheel in front of her, making us SPIN even faster.

                         LESTER (V.O.)
                     (with love)
                And... Carolyn.

EXT. PARKING LOT - DAY

**On VIDEO:** We're watching the video Ricky showed Jane earlier, of the empty white PLASTIC BAG being blown about. The wind carries it in a circle around us, sometimes whipping it about violently, or, without warning, sending it soaring skyward, then letting it float gracefully down to the ground...

                  LESTER (V.O.)
I guess I could be pretty pissed off about what happened to me... but it's hard to stay mad, when there's so much beauty in the world. Sometimes I feel like I'm seeing it all at once, and it's too much, my heart fills up like a balloon that's about to burst...

EXT. - ROBIN HOOD TRAIL - DAY

We're FLYING once again over Robin Hood Trail, ASCENDING SLOWLY.

                  LESTER (V.O.)
...and then I remember to relax, and stop trying to hold on to it, and then it flows through me like rain and I can't feel anything but gratitude for every single moment of my stupid little life...
        (amused)
You have no idea what I'm talking about, I'm sure. But don't worry...

FADE TO BLACK.

                  LESTER (V.O.)
You will someday.

# STILLS

Kevin Spacey stars as Lester Burnham, who is about to make some major changes in his typical suburban life.

Annette Bening, as Carolyn Burnham, in her perfect suburban rose garden.

*Top:* Thora Birch as the Burnham's teenage daughter Jane.
*Bottom:* Wes Bentley plays Ricky Fitts, who is not your typical boy next door.

*Top:* Mena Suvari plays Angela, the teenage beauty who becomes the object of Lester's desires. *Bottom:* Chris Cooper gives a hard-edged portrayal of the strict Colonel Fitts.

*Top:* A hapless Lester Burnham heads off to work.
*Bottom:* Jim *(Sam Robards)* and his partner Jim *(Scott Bakula)* welcome Colonel Fitts to the neighborhood.

*Top:* Jane and Angela have very different reactions to the new kid in town, Ricky Fitts.
*Bottom:* Lester tries in vain to communicate with his daughter Jane.

*Top:* Jane finds herself increasingly intrigued by Ricky.
*Bottom:* Ricky focuses his attentions and his video camera on Jane.

*Top:* Kevin Spacey and Annette Bening star as Lester and Carolyn Burnham, an estranged sub–
urban couple at a crossroads in their relationship.
*Bottom:* Carolyn finds personal and professional inspiration in Buddy Kane, the "King of Real
Estate," played by Peter Gallagher.

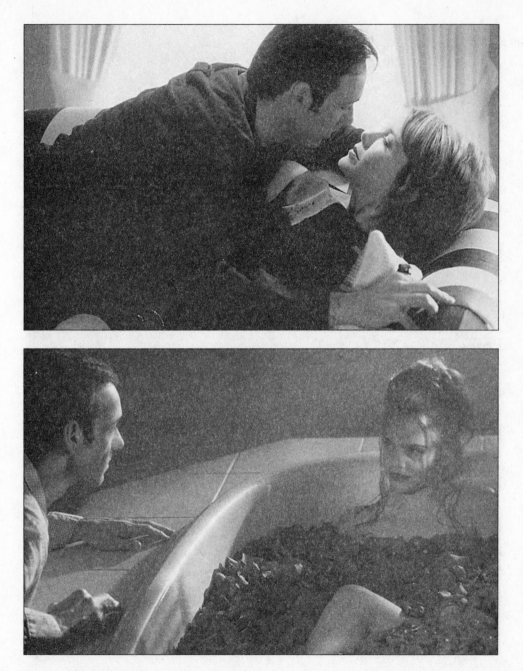

*Top:* Lester tries to reignite sparks with Carolyn.
*Bottom:* Lester has a growing fascination with the beautiful young Angela.

Lester finds job satisfaction in his new career as a burger boy at Mr. Smiley's.

Determined to make a sale, Carolyn prepares for an open house.

*Top:* On a rainy night, Lester and Colonel Fitts have a climactic encounter in Lester's garage. *Bottom:* Director Sam Mendes discusses a scene with Annette Bening and Kevin Spacey.

# AFTERWORD

# BY ALAN BALL

I think the idea for *American Beauty* first started rattling around in my head during the whole Amy Fisher/Joey Buttafuoco drama. I was a playwright living in New York, working in the art department of a magazine in midtown Manhattan. On my lunch break one day, I passed a street vendor selling a comic book version of Amy and Joey's story. The cover featured a drawing of a demonic-looking Joey (with a pronounced beer gut) seducing a virginal Amy; on the flip side was an alternate cover with a good Catholic (and much slimmer) Joey spurning the advances of a furious and vindictive Amy as slut from hell. Inside were two equally differing comic-strip accounts of what had happened. This was right after the news had broken of those sad events on Long Island, long before the TV movies started appearing.

I had been just as fascinated, repulsed, and entertained by those events as everyone else, but as I stood there leafing through that comic book, it struck me: we would never know what really happened. The media circus had already begun, and the story was swiftly being reduced to its most lurid elements, with a cast of cardboard stock characters acting on their basest impulses. But underneath it all were real human lives that had gone horribly astray. What had become fodder for jokes on late-night talk shows was to those who had lived it genuine tragedy—and, no doubt, a far more complicated and interesting story than any we would ever hear.

That realization—and an encounter with a plastic bag outside the World Trade Center—was the basis for what would eventually become *American Beauty*. I first started to write it as a play, in which Jane actually did hire Ricky to kill her father because she felt he was just too, well, embarrassing. But it didn't feel right, and after twenty or so pages, I abandoned it. Years later, after moving to Los Angeles and spending four seasons as a sitcom writer, I started working on it again, this time as a screenplay. Before I knew it, it was all I could think about; I couldn't wait to get a chance to work on it. Even if I got home at 3 A.M. (as sitcom writers often do), I'd immediately sit down at the computer and work, sometimes till dawn. It was as if the story had a life of its own, and all I had to do was transcribe it.

I had heard nothing but horror stories of other screenwriters' experiences when their scripts were produced, but I can honestly say that for me the filming of *American Beauty* was a joy. Sam Mendes is not only a brilliant director, he's incredibly generous and collaborative, and coming from the theater, considers the writer to be an intrinsic part of the process. I was on the set almost every day. One of the most productive times for me (and for the script) was a two-week rehearsal period with the actors prior to filming; they brought depth to the characters I had never imagined, and their insights and suggestions helped immensely.

But eventually, the film began to acquire its own life, just as the screenplay had when I was writing it. Portions of scenes that seemed vitally important on the page suddenly lost their impact, or felt like they were from another movie. Entire sequences were shot, only to be excised later. As Sam observed during editing, "It's like the movie is letting us know what it wants to be." The script contained in this book is the script to that film, the film that *American Beauty* became—a better film than the one I originally wrote. What started out as a satire of middle-class American values in the media age eventually revealed itself to be something entirely different, and much more interesting, just like most of the characters in the film. I cannot begin to claim credit for that; it must be shared with Sam, an amazing cast, producers Dan Jinks and Bruce Cohen, DreamWorks, and every single member of the crew.

We live in such a manufactured culture, one that thrives on simplifying and packaging experience quickly so it can be sold. But as Ricky knows—and Lester learns—things are infinitely deeper and richer than they appear on the surface. And although the puritanical would have us believe otherwise, there is room for beauty in every facet of existence.

# BIOGRAPHIES

**ALAN BALL** (Screenwriter/Co-Producer) won the 1999 Academy Award® for Best Original Screenplay, along with a Golden Globe and the Writers Guild of America award, for *American Beauty*, which he counts as his first produced feature film script. He enjoyed similar success with his critically lauded HBO drama *Six Feet Under*, winner of the Golden Globe for Best Television Series. He was the series' creator and executive producer, and wrote several episodes, including the pilot and "An Open Book."

Previously, Ball wrote for the hit series *Cybill* for three seasons, eventually becoming co-executive producer. He first made his name in television when he was offered a job writing for *Grace Under Fire* after producing partners Tom Werner and Marcy Carsey read one of his plays.

Prior to moving to Hollywood, Ball was a playwright in New York. Among his credits are *Five Women Wearing the Same Dress*, which premiered in 1993 at Manhattan Class Company and starred Thomas Gibson, Ally Walker, and Allison Janney; *The M Word*, which premiered at the inaugural Lucille Ball Festival of New American Comedy in 1991; *Made For a Woman*; *Bachelor Holiday*; *The Amazing Adventures of Tense Guy*; *Your Mother's Butt*; *Power Lunch*; and *The Two Mrs. Trumps*.

Born in Atlanta, Ball was raised in Marietta, Georgia. He attended Florida State University, where he majored in theater with an emphasis in acting and playwriting. After college he moved to New York City, where he worked as an art director at *Adweek* and *Inside PR* magazines.

**SAM MENDES** (Director), one of today's most celebrated theater directors, has mounted award-winning productions on the stages of London, New York, and around the world. With *American Beauty*, his feature film directorial debut, he won an Oscar® and a Golden Globe for Best Director, as well as the Directors Guild of America award for Outstanding Directorial Achievement in Motion Pictures.

Mendes's many triumphs include the acclaimed revival of the musical *Cabaret*, first in London and then on Broadway. The latter production garnered four Tony Awards, including one for Best Revival of a Musical, three Drama Desk Awards, and three Outer Critics Circle Awards. He also directed *The Blue Room* on Broadway, starring Nicole Kidman. Mendes had previously directed the award-winning London production of *The Rise and Fall of Little Voice*, introducing Jane Horrocks, who reprised her role in the film version, *Little Voice*.

Born in England, Mendes was educated at Cambridge University and joined the Chichester Festival Theatre following his graduation in 1987. Soon after, he directed Dame Judi Dench in *The Cherry Orchard*, for which he won a Critics Circle Award for Best Newcomer. He then joined the Royal Shakespeare Company in 1990, where he directed such productions as *Troilus and Cressida* with Ralph Fiennes, *Richard III*, and *The Tempest*, for which he earned an Olivier Award nomination.

In 1992, Mendes became artistic director of the reopened Donmar Warehouse in London. There he has directed numerous award-winning productions, including the aforementioned *Cabaret*, and *The Glass Menagerie* and *Company*, for each of which he won the Olivier Award for Best Director. His other work at the Donmar includes *Assassins*, which won a Critics Circle Award, *Translations*, *Glengarry Glen Ross*, *Habeas Corpus*, and *The Front Page*.

Mendes's most recent films include *Road to Perdition* and *Jarhead*. He also directed a revival of the Stephen Sondheim musical *Gypsy*, starring actress Bernadette Peters.

# CAST AND CREW CREDITS

DREAMWORKS PICTURES presents

A JINKS/COHEN COMPANY PRODUCTION

KEVIN SPACEY        ANNETTE BENING

## AMERICAN BEAUTY

THORA BIRCH     WES BENTLEY     MENA SUVARI

PETER GALLAGHER    ALLISON JANNEY    SCOTT BAKULA    SAM ROBARDS

and CHRIS COOPER

| | | |
|---|---|---|
| *Directed by*<br>SAM MENDES | *Written by*<br>ALAN BALL | *Produced by*<br>BRUCE COHEN<br>& DAN JINKS |
| *Director of Photography*<br>CONRAD L. HALL, A.S.C. | *Production Designer*<br>NAOMI SHOHAN | |
| | | *Edited by*<br>TARIQ ANWAR<br>CHRIS GREENBURY |
| *Casting by*<br>DEBRA ZANE, C.S.A. | *Costume Designer*<br>JULIE WEISS | |
| *Music Supervisor*<br>CHRIS DOURIDAS | *Co-Producers*<br>STAN WLODKOWSKI<br>ALAN BALL | *Music by*<br>THOMAS NEWMAN |

## CAST

| | |
|---|---|
| Lester Burnham . . . . . . . . . . . . . . . . . . KEVIN SPACEY | Spartanette #3 . . . . . . . . . . . . . . . . . LILY HOUTKIN |
| Carolyn Burnham . . . . . . . . . . . . . . ANNETTE BENING | Spartanette #4 . . . . . . . . . . . . . CAROLINA LANCASTER |
| Jane Burnham . . . . . . . . . . . . . . . . . THORA BIRCH | Spartanette #5 . . . . . . . . . . . . . . . . . ROMANA LEAH |
| Ricky Fitts . . . . . . . . . . . . . . . . . . . WES BENTLEY | Spartanette #6 . . . . . . . . . . . . CHEKESA VAN PUTTEN |
| Angela Hayes. . . . . . . . . . . . . . . . . MENA SUVARI | Spartanette #7 . . . . . . . . . . . . . . . . EMILY ZACHARY |
| Buddy Kane . . . . . . . . . . . . . . PETER GALLAGHER | Spartanette #8 . . . . . . . . . . . . . . . NANCY ANDERSON |
| Barbara Fitts . . . . . . . . . . . . . . . . ALLISON JANNEY | Spartanette #9 . . . . . . . . . . . . . . . . RESHMA GAJJAR |
| Colonel Fitts. . . . . . . . . . . . . . . . . CHRIS COOPER | Spartanette #10 . . . . . . . . . . . . . . STEPHANIE RIZZO |
| Jim #1 . . . . . . . . . . . . . . . . . . . . SCOTT BAKULA | Teenage Girl #1 . . . . . . . . . . . . . HEATHER JOY SHER |
| Jim #2. . . . . . . . . . . . . . . . . . . . SAM ROBARDS | Teenage Girl #2 . . . . . . . . . CHELSEA HERTFORD |
| Brad . . . . . . . . . . . . . . . BARRY DEL SHERMAN | Christy Kane . . . . . . . . . . . . . . . . . AMBER SMITH |
| Sale House Woman #1 . . . . . . . . . . . ARA CELI | Catering Boss. . . . . . . . . . . . . . . . JOEL McCRARY |
| Sale House Man #1 . . . . . . . . . . . . . JOHN CHO | Mr. Smiley's Counter Girl (Janine) MARISSA JARET WINOKUR |
| Sale House Man #2 . . . . . . . . . FORT ATKINSON | Mr. Smiley's Manager . . . . . . . . . DENNIS ANDERSON |
| Sale House Woman #2. . . . . . . . . . . SUE CASEY | Firing Range Attendant . . . . . . . MATTHEW KIMBROUGH |
| Sale House Man #3 . . . . . . . . . . KENT FAULCON | Young Jane . . . . . . . . . ERIN CATHRYN STRUBBE |
| Sale House Women #4 . . . . . . . . BRENDA WEHLE | Stunt Coordinator. . . . . . . . . . . . . . . BEN SCOTT |
| LISA CLOUD | Utility Stunt. . . . . . . . . . . . . . . . . PHIL CULOTTA |
| Spartanette #1. . . . . . . . . . . . . . . ALISON FAULK | Pilot . . . . . . . . . . . . . . . . . ROBERT ZAJONC |
| Spartanette #2 . . . . . . . . . . . . . KRISTA GOODSITT | |

Unit Production Manager
CRISTEN CARR STRUBBE

First Assistant Directors
TONY ADLER
CAREY DIETRICH

Second Assistant Director
ROSEMARY CREMONA

Choreographer
PAULA ABDUL

# CREW

Art Director . . . . . . . . . . . . . . . . . DAVID S. LAZAN
Assistant Art Director . . . . . . . . . . CATHERINE SMITH
Set Decorator . . . . . . . . . JAN K. BERGSTROM, S.D.S.A.
Camera Operator . . . . . . . . . . . . . . . AARON PAZANTI
First Assistant Camera . . . . . . . . . . . CLYDE E. BRYAN
Second Assistant Camera . . . . . . . SUZANNE M. TRUCKS
Camera Loader . . . . . . . . . . . . . MICHAEL THOMAS
Still Photographer . . . . . . . . . . . . LOREY SEBASTIAN
Script Supervisor . . . . . . . . . . ANA MARIA QUINTANA
Supervising Sound Editor  SCOTT MARTIN GERSHIN, M.P.S.E.
Re-Recording Mixers . . SCOTT MILLAN and BOB BEEMER
Production Sound Mixer . . . . . . . RICHARD VAN DYKE
Boom Operator . . . . . . . . . . . . . . . CARL FISHER
Video Camera Operator . . . . . . . . . GEOFFREY HALEY
Chief Lighting Technician . . . . . . . . . . . . TOM STERN
Assistant Chief Lighting Technician . . . . . . JOHN CARNEY
Rigging Gaffer . . . . . . . . . . . . HUSTON BEAUMONT
Electricians . . . . . . . . . . . . . . . . . LESTER BOYKIN
ROSS DUNKERLEY
EARL GAYER
JOHN LACY
DAVID NEALE
ANDY TOWNE
Key Grip . . . . . . . . . . . . . . . . . . . BILL YOUNG
Best Boy Grips . . . . . . . . . . . . . . . . . . DON VOS
DEAN KING
Dolly Grip . . . . . . . . . . . . . . CARLOS GALLARDO
Rigging Key Grip . . . . . . . . . . . . . . . JERRY KING
Grips
TOM BOONE              JOHN EMORY
RON GLENN             THOMAS NOROIAN
Property Master . . . . . . . . . . . . . . . LYNDA REISS
Assistant Property Master . . . . . . . . ANGELA WHITING
Special Effects Coordinator . . . . . . . JOHN C. HARTIGAN
Special Effects Assistants . . . . . . . . . . . . . . . . . . .
JASON HANSEN              WAYNE INCORVAIA
GENE RIZZARDI             PAUL SOKOL
MICHAEL THOMPSON   CHRISTOPHER WALKOWIAK
Costume Supervisor . . . . . . . . . . . . HOPE B. SLEPAK
Assistant Costume Designer . . . . . . . MARCY FROEHLICH
Key Costumer . . . . . . . . . . . . . . SANFORD SLEPAK
Set Costumers . . . . . . . . . . . . . . . . ALIX HESTER
. KANANI WOLF
Key Makeup Artist . . . . . . . . . . . . TANIA McCOMAS
Makeup Artist . . . . . . . . . . CHRISTINE M. STEELE

Ms. Bening's Makeup Artist . . . . . . . . . . JULIE HEWETT
Key Hair Stylist . . . . . . . . . . . CAROL A. O'CONNELL
Hair Stylist . . . . . . . . . . PATRICIA DEHANEY-LE MAY
Ms. Bening's Hair Stylist . . . . . . . . . . CYDNEY CORNELL
Production Coordinator . . . . . . . CHRISTA VAUSBINDER
Assistant Production Coordinator . . . . SHANNON SPEAKER
Production Secretary . . . . . . . . . . . . . MATT WALKER
Production Controller . . . . . . . . . . . . . JIM TURNER
Production Accountant . . . . . . . . . . JANET LONSDALE
Assistant Accountants . . . . . . . . . . . . TRICIA KINGERY
VICTOR HADDOX
Payroll Accountant . . . . . . . . . DEBBIE LYNN SIEGEL
Post Production Accountant . . . . . . . . MARIA DeVANE
Location Manager . . . . . . . . . . . CHRISTINE BONNEM
Key Assistant Location Manager . . . . . . YOSHI ENOKI, JR.
Locations Assistant . . . . . . . . . . . . . . . . CHEE HO
Second Assistant Director . . . . . . . . PETER E. HIRSCH
Second Second Assistant Director . . . . . STEPHANIE KIME
Casting Assistant . . . . . . . . . . . . . . . TERRI TAYLOR
Extras Casting . . . . . . . . . . . . . . RAQUEL OSBORNE
Assistant Choreographer . . . . . . . . . . CINDY PICKER
Unit Publicist . . . . . . . . . . . . . . . . . DAVID LINCK
Art Department Coordinator . . . . . . . . . MOLLY CLICK
Set Decoration Coordinator . . . . . . . LISA PENARANDA
Set Designers . . . . . . . . . . . . . . . ANDREA DOPASO
SUZAN WEXLER
Storyboard Artists . . . . . . . . . . . ROBIN RICHESSON
TONY CHANCE
Leadpersons . . . . . . . . . . . . . . MICHAEL P. CASEY
MICHAEL HIGELMIRE
Swing Gang . . . . . . . . . . . . . . . . BROOK BACON
KEVIN CHAMBERS
GARY KUDROFF
JOHN A. SCOTT III
On-Set Dressers . . . . . . . . . . . . . CAROLYN LASSEK
IAN KAY
Researcher . . . . . . . . . . . . . . DEBORAH RICKETTS
Construction Coordinator . . . . . . . . . JOE ONDREJKO
Propmaker Foreman . . . . . . . . . . . ROBERT GARLOW
Paint Foreman . . . . . . . . . . . . . . TOM HRUPCHO
Plasterer Foreman . . . . . . . . . . . . . JIM HERITAGE
Greens Foreman . . . . . . . . . . . RICHARD W. JONES
Standby Painter . . . . . . . . . . . . CHRIS ZIMMERMAN
Transportation Coordinator . . . . . . A. WELCH LAMBETH
Transportation Captain . . . . . . . . RANDY LOVELADY
Drivers
JEFF COUCH                ED EVANS
JIM JOHNSON               AL KAMINSKY
RON LINXWILER           GEORGE R. MATEJKA
HECTOR MENDOZA        WAYNE PARVIAINEN
GLEN R. POLZEL          DANIEL ROUTHIEAUX
PAUL SCHWANKE          TYLER TENNESEN
JON THORGUSEN            DAVE TREVINO
DANIEL VALENZUELA         BILL WOLFF
PRENTIS WOODS          MARK YACULLO
Craft Service . . . . . . . . . . CHARLES "BILLY" WEAVER
Caterer . . . . . . . . . . . . . . . . . . . . . . DELUXE
Animal Handler . . . . . . . . . . . . . . JOY A. GREEN

Studio Teacher . . . . . . . . . . . . . . . . . . PIA MEHR
24-Frame Video Playback . . . . . . . . . . . . . . . $E=mc^2$
24-Frame Video Playback Technician . . JENNIFER CARLSON
Assistant to Mr. Mendes . . . . . . . . . . . TARA B. COOK
Assistant to Mr. Cohen & Mr. Jinks . . . . . . KELLY STUART
Assistant to Ms. Bening . . . . . . . . . . KIM MOZINGO
Assistants to Mr. Spacey . . . . . . . . . . . . . . . .
   MIKE WELCH              DANA BRUNETTI
Personal Trainer to Mr. Spacey . . . . . . . . MIKE TORCHIA
Production Assistants . . . . . . . . . . . . . . . . .
   STEVEN BUHAI      STEPHEN P. DEL PRETE
   MAURICE "MOE" FREEMAN    ANNA E. HAYWARD
   JEFFREY JENOFSKY     MARK RABINOWITZ
   J. BEN SYKES     GEORGE L. TARRANT, JR.
   CHRISTIAN WALSH   GILLIAN MARTIN WATERMAN
Stand-Ins . . . . . . . . . . . . . . . . . . . .
   MARINA FREEMAN     NICHOLE McWHORTER
   DAMON PRESTON     DANIEL J. WALSH
First Aid . . . . . . . . . . . . . . . TIMOTHY J. WERLE
                ROBERT BRUGGER
Construction First Aid. . . . . . . . . . LANCE MANCUSO
Post Production Executive. . . . . . . . . . MARTIN COHEN
Post Production Supervisor . . . . . . LISA DENNIS KENNEDY
Post Production Coordinator. . . . . . . LISA MARIE SERRA
First Assistant Editors . . . . . . TRACEY WADMORE-SMITH
                LARRY MADARAS
Avid Assistants . . . . . . . . . . . . . . VINCE FILIPPONE
                P.J. HARLING
Editorial Production Assistant . . . . . . . JEFFREY SKINNER
Projectionist . . . . . . . . . . . . . . RENE GONZALES
First Assistant Sound Editor . THOMAS O'NEIL YOUNKMAN
ADR Supervisor . . . . . . . . . . . . . TREVOR JOLLY
Dialogue Editors . . . . . . . . . . . . . . . . SIMON COKE
                MARK GORDON
Sound Effects Editors . . . . . . . . . . . ALAN RANKIN
                BRYAN BOWEN
Foley Editors . . . . . . . . . . . . . . . PETER ZINDA
                TOM OZANICH
Digital Sound Assistants . . . . . . . . PAUL FLINCHBAUGH
                LEE LeBAIGUE
ADR Mixers . . . . . . . . . . . . RICHARD WEINGART
                DEAN DRABIN
ADR Recordist. . . . . . . . . . . . . . BRIAN BASHAM
Foley Artists . . . . . . . . . . . . JEFFREY B. WILHOIT
                JAMES MORIANA
Foley Mixer . . . . . . . . . . . . . NERSES GEZALYAN
Foley Recordist . . . . . . . . . . . . GREG ZIMMERMAN
Additional Audio . . . . . . . . . . . MARK ORMANDY
ADR Voice Casting . . . . . . . . . . . . . L.A. MadDogs
Re-Recorded at . . . . . . . . . . . . . . TODD-AO WEST
Executive in Charge of Music . . . . . . . . TODD HOMME
Music Editors . . . . . . . . . . . . . BILL BERNSTEIN
                JOANIE DIENER
Assistant Music Editor . . . . . . . . JORDAN CORNGOLD
Titles & Opticals. . . . . . . PACIFIC TITLE RESEARCH
Avid Equipment by. . . . . . . . . . . . . . . . . DES
Negative Cutter . . . . . . . . . . . . KONA CUTTING
Color Timer . . . . . . . . . . . . . . . PHIL HETO

Camera Cranes & Dollies by . . . . . . . . . . . . . . .
CHAPMAN/LEONARD STUDIO EQUIPMENT, INC.

## SECOND UNIT

First Assistant Director . . . . . . . . . . CHRIS EDMONDS
Second Assistant Director. . . MICHELLE MUGGS EDMONDS
Directors of Photography . . . . . . . . CONRAD HALL, JR.
                DAVID GOLIA
First Assistant Camera . . . . . . . . . . . . DAVID RILEY
Second Assistant Camera. . . . . . . . . . . MIKE GENTILE
Script Supervisor . . . . . . . MARILYN GIARDINO-ZYEH
Visual Effects Gaffer. . . . . . . . . . . . JAMES McEWEN
Chief Lighting Technician . . . . . . . . . . . JAMES COX
Assistant Chief Lighting Technician . . . . PATRICK RALSTON
Key Grip . . . . . . . . . . . . . . . . KENNY KING
Best Boy Grip . . . . . . . . . . . . . . PAUL FARLEY
Dolly Grip . . . . . . . . SERGIO "PONCH" GUTIERREZ
Set Costumer . . . . . . . . . . . . . . LEE HARRIS
Makeup Artist . . . . . . . . . . . . JULIET LOVELAND
Hair Stylists . . . . . . . . . . . . . . . CHERI RUFF
                STEVE R. SOUSSANA
24-Frame Playback Technician. . . . . . RALPH MERZBACH
Craft Service . . . . . . . . . . . . . . KRISSY KORN
Production Assistants . . . . . . . . . . MIKE MUSTERIC
                MICHAEL LABOG

Special Visual Effects by
CFC/MVFX, Los Angeles
Supervisors . . . . . . . . . . . . . . . . ROB HODGSON
                DAVID GOLDBERG
Producers . . . . . . . . . . . . . . . . JANET YALE
              JONATHAN F. STYRLUND
Compositors . . . . . . . . . . . FORTUNATO FRATTASIO
              MATT DESSERO
3d Artists . . . . . . . . . . . . ROBERT CHAPIN
              JOHN CASSELLA, JR.
Paint/Roto Artists. . . . . . . . . . . . SUSAN EVANS
              NICOLLE CORNUTE
              TOMME B. STANLEY
Editorial . . . . . . . . . . . . MATT MAGNOLIA
Technical Assistants . . . . . . . . . . . . JENNY BEHNKE
              SHELDON RAMONES
              DAVID DURHAM
              NICOLLE GRAY
Runner . . . . . . . . . . . . . . . JOHN BOZZALLA
Managing Director . . . . . . . . . . . . . . DON FLY

Special Thanks to
PETE TOWNSHEND

Thanks to
ALL AT THE DONMAR WAREHOUSE IN LONDON
DR. BILL AND ALICE

FILMED AT WARNER BROS. STUDIOS,
BURBANK, CALIFORNIA